THE Point

LORI THOMAS HARRINGTON

BLUE TULIP
PUBLISHING

The Point
By Lori Thomas Harrington
Blue Tulip Publishing
www.bluetulippublishing.com

This is a work of fiction. Names, places, characters, and events are fictitious in every regard. Any similarities to actual events and persons, living or dead, are purely coincidental. Any trademarks, service marks, product names, or named features are assumed to be the property of their respective owners, and are used only for reference. There is no implied endorsement if any of these terms are used. Except for review purposes, the reproduction of this book in whole or part, electronically or mechanically, constitutes a copyright violation.

THE POINT
Copyright © 2016 LORI THOMAS HARRINGTON
ISBN-13: 978-1539006145
ISBN-10: 153900614X
Cover Art by Jena Brignola

For Hank,
the love of my life

Prologue

"You cannot find peace by avoiding life."
~Virginia Woolf

AT THE TIME of its former glory, the Sinclair Hastings Plantation must have been an incredible sight. What now lay in ruins certainly held secrets of days past—some of which Emma Ashby knew. Though her own secrets lingered in the place, they didn't date as far back as the mid 1800's when the home was established, but her soul remained bound to the place just the same. Just sitting on the grounds, breathing the air, and absorbing the surroundings proved enough to transport her back—even now. She drifted back to a place where so much life happened—a place where lifetime friendships originated — a place where young imaginations soared as high as the hill in Leyton, TN where the majestic Hastings' home once resided. In this very place, love blossomed—the same place where love was lost.

In the stillness, a hush blanketed the place. To her, this setting transcended life as she had known it. Even now, it served as a catalyst to penetrate a place in her heart that remained sealed until this moment. Today the seal broke, and she was confident that the flood of memories would overtake her.

She closed her eyes and tasted Drew's salty tears. She felt his breath in her lungs from the last day they spent together. Standing on the threshold where shadows of yesterday taunted her, the familiar ache returned deep within her soul. She longed for just one day—one more day to play, to laugh, and to be a child again. If only she could be free from the cares of her world now—to be herself, free to love with all her heart—free to love Drew.

Emma suddenly snapped back into the present, realizing those days had long passed. The finality occurred under the setting of an August sun on a day that seemed like a lifetime ago. She stared at the old gazebo, which was built around the well house where she and Drew had played for hours. In the distance, she saw the special place where all her hopes originated and then died under that starry sky many summers ago. The old Sinclair Hastings mansion was not appealing to most, but to Emma and Drew, it was a beautiful castle. Together, they saw the splendor and magic that dwelt around the place. They always had hopes to make it come alive again so everyone could see it. She sighed and whispered, "Home again for the dedication of Hastings Hall."

For years, the Dalton family dreamed of constructing Hastings Hall—especially Drew's mother, Liza Dalton. Until now, it didn't seem feasible. Several acres separated the new structure and the old mansion. Drew's great, great grandfather, James Sinclair Hastings, owned the land in the beginning. It remained in Drew's mother's family for generations, and Liza Hastings Dalton wanted to build something as a memorial to him that would benefit the community. As children, Emma and Drew used the grounds as their playground. Now, the time had changed that, too.

Emma was amazed when her mom shared how the little town had grown over the past few years. Living in Alabama, she didn't make it home as often as she thought she would when she first took her job at an advertising agency in Tuscaloosa. The small town of Leyton, with the growing population up to 8,526, according to the latest census count, had been in dire need of a banquet hall of such caliber for some time. The nearby town of Pulaski was too far to drive for a wedding reception, birthday party, or anything along the lines of a nice celebration.

The truth was, this sleepy little town was about to die until the strangest thing happened. Young people moved back home after the economy took a turn for the worse. Small family-owned businesses that looked as if they would die with the present generation made a comeback. The little city of Leyton, TN had changed. Coming back home suddenly seemed to be a great idea—the perfect place to raise a family—if you were into that kind of thing.

Of course, as different as things were, some things would never change. As she walked back to her Jeep Wrangler, Emma reminded herself that she chose to put the past behind her. Since graduating from the University of Alabama, she had concentrated on her, and that, by far, was what she did best. Although she had always dreamed of writing a great novel and living in the Hastings Mansion as the wife of Drew Dalton, she was grateful for the job she landed just out of college with Barlow and Stallings Advertising Agency.

She felt like she gave up the possibility of those dreams coming true a lifetime ago. Even though she started out as an intern at the agency, she was soon recognized as the fresh new talent. Back then she had no desire to do anything other than work. Work took her mind off life—a life without Drew. No matter how many years passed, the ache and longing remained inside her soul even though that loss was just a distant memory. Her plan to suffocate her pain with her job had worked fine until now—exactly seven years later.

As she climbed into her jeep and drove away, she took one last look in her rearview mirror and wondered if looking at her past through her own eyes hurt this much, *how much more will it hurt to look into Drew's eyes?*

On this trip, she couldn't avoid seeing him, and the dreadful meeting would occur in less than twenty-four hours. She was surprisingly nervous that her past was about to collide with her present.

Chapter One

"All changes are more or less tinged with melancholy, for what we are leaving behind is part of ourselves."
~Amelia Barr

ALL DAY, DREW Dalton tried to keep himself occupied. Working out kinks in the sound system at Hastings Hall proved to be a good way to accomplish this. As one mishap after the other occurred, his mother bombarded him with last-minute tasks. Because his profession was a sound engineer, he had meticulously chosen the best available sound system. He knew how important this project was to his family, and his mother was thrilled that he volunteered to handle the sound equipment.

However, like every true southern mama, Liza Dalton had other intentions. She knew that Drew was engaged, but she couldn't shake the feeling that he and Emma Ashby had unfinished issues to work through.

Drew's sister, Julie, was ten years older than him, and by Drew's eighth grade year, she had married and moved to Pulaski, TN, about fifty miles away. Just after their first anniversary, she and her husband, John Benjamin Scott, opened a clothing store. The Knit Whit was extremely successful, and they soon had to hire additional help. They hired Darby Spencer immediately. Although she started working at the store while she was still in high school, she soon became Julie's right hand. After graduating college, Darby returned to the store, worked as an assistant to Julie, and became a buyer for the growing company.

Like Liza, Julie wanted her little brother to move on with his life and stop living in the past. After he and Emma parted ways, he never seriously dated anyone. Julie finally got Drew to agree to meet Darby, and two years later, they were engaged to be married.

Liza felt she had a small window of opportunity, so she hired Ella Ashby to decorate for the exquisite dedication. She knew Ella would ask her daughter to help with a job of that magnitude. She also knew how close the two families had always been, so she was sure that Emma would come home for the dedication. Now, it was only a matter of time before Drew and Emma would have to deal with their past. No matter the repercussion, Liza knew it was time to deal with it and put the past to rest. This meeting was long overdue. Liza didn't think they would arrange a meeting on their own, and she was confident that Drew couldn't truly move on without some closure, so she gave them a little nudge.

"Mom, don't let anyone near my equipment. I'm going to pick up a couple mic stands, but I'll be back in a couple of hours. Need anything?"

Holding her hand up as if to put him on pause, she continued her phone conversation. As he listened, he knew he was about to regret his offer. Liza Dalton hung up the phone and, with a smile, answered her son. "Why, yes. I need you to run this by Petals for me. El's in the shop now, and I don't trust her teenage worker to remember to give it to her, so drop it off first, please."

She knew her son didn't expect that task. She laughed to herself watching his facial expression. It was clear the thought of going inside the florist shop shook him a little. He adored Mama El. She was a second mom to him, but since Emma left, the hurt won out all too often, and he chose to distance himself from the shop.

"Sure. Anything else?" he asked hesitantly.

She smiled. "Nope. That's it. Oh, wait—there is one more thing. Pick me up some lunch?" Then, with a wink, she added, "The regular."

He shook his head, agreed, and waved. When he finally got into his maroon '63 Mustang, he closed the door and sat in the silence. He ran his fingers through his hair and took in a deep breath. He could only think of one thing—Emma.

Before making her way to Flower Petals and Gifts, Emma stopped by the Mazi Daze Café, Mazi's for short. She knew her mom well enough to know that there would be no letting up when crunch time set in. Besides, it had been some time since her last trip home and she wanted to see Ms. Mazi. Not to mention, she craved her regular order of the past—Ms. Mazi's amazing chicken salad with a large unsweetened tea— with extra ice. In the south, everyone drank sweet tea, but not Emma, so Ms. Mazi always joked with Emma about her "drinking problem."

As she entered the café, she lost herself to memories. One of the greatest attractions about the café was the legendary "wall of fame" or "wall of shame" as most people referred to it. Mazi McCarty had pictures, signatures, quotes, and all sorts of tidbits on the back wall of the establishment, which had been a booming business even during the hard times. A collection of over thirty years' worth of friends graced the doors of the place.

Emma laughed seeing the picture of Della Reece from the television series, *Touched by an Angel*. Upon passing through Leyton, Ms. Reece had car trouble. She had to wait most of the day on repairs, and the entire town was in a stir over her presence in the small town. It even made it on the local news that night.

Emma's laughter ended when she noticed the picture beside it. Emma's heart fell as she spotted a picture of her and Drew holding the award for most original homecoming skit their senior year of high school. Soon, a smile fell over her as she recalled the day they made the front page of the *Leyton Daily Times* that September in 2004.

"Okay you two, show some school spirit." Snap. Snap. Snap. Emma remembered how hard she laughed as Drew swept her up and cradled her into his muscular arms while she held hers arms out, striking a pose. *"Put me down, Drew. The picture's over. Put me down."* She could barely speak from laughing so hard. He refused to let her go until she admitted that his mad editing skills landed the win for them. She held her ground. *"My killer parody of 'Benny and the Jets' brought us the victory."* In between her pleading for mercy and kicking in the air, he tickled her relentlessly. *"Say I*

am the mastermind. Say it's me, Em. Say it." In between tickles and taunting, he stole small kisses.

Still lost in thought, she heard a familiar voice behind her say, "Say it, Em. Say it's me."

For a moment, she couldn't find her next breath. She finally managed to turn around. He had dark brown hair, deep ocean-blue eyes, and perfect bone structure. He obviously had been working out, and he looked better than she remembered. She inhaled his scent, and she felt his piercing eyes invade her. Finally, upon finding her voice, she forced herself to speak. "Drew Dalton, how long has it been?" she asked, leaning in to give him a safe, brief hug. *Oh great. I'm sure I have red blotches all over my chest.*

AFTER RELUCTANTLY PULLING away Drew said, "Hi, Emma. It has been a while. You look great. How have you been?"

She told him about her job, and he briefly told her about his work at the radio station.

Before he walked over to speak to Emma, he had been standing at a distance looking at her across the room. He'd fought the urge to turn and walk out of the café as if he never saw her. She still had the ability to pull him toward her—like gravity. Helplessly, he walked directly over to her—fumbling for words as he gazed into her familiar hazel eyes. Now he was finally able to breathe like a normal person and started telling her about his business he had on the side. Unfortunately, the girl behind the counter let him know his order was ready.

After pausing briefly, Drew turned to her and softly spoke. "It's good to see you again, Em." With a nod and soft brushing of his hand on her forearm, he turned and walked away.

Drew quickly delivered the sandwich to his mom and assured her the list was safe in Mrs. Ella's hands. He made an excuse about the microphone stands he had planned to pick up, but the truth was that after seeing Emma, he could hardly think of anything else. He only wanted to leave and go to the only place where he could make sense of his world. He called it "The Point." It was actually *the highest* point in Leyton, so the name was a given. He and Emma deemed it their place long ago when they were in grammar school. Though they called it The Point, when they were in junior high, they decided to combine their last names, Ashby and Dalton, to give it an official name—'Ashton Point.'

He parked at the front of what was left of the old mansion. It was in poor condition now, and had been for many years. The roof had water damage, which caused the staircase to rot out, making the second floor inaccessible. The paint had not fared well throughout the years either. The shutters were barely hanging. Although it had aged over the years, the structure was solid, and that was all that mattered to Drew. He saw past the flaws and saw the beauty that remained. The grand stone steps leading to the front porch, the detail in the four stone columns across the front of the house, and the unique style of the old plantation home still captured his heart and his sense of wonder.

He had hoped it wouldn't catch the heart of his mother. Secretly, he always wished that he and Emma could renovate it and bring it back to life so they could live there, but the days of those dreams were long gone. Too much time had passed. He knew he would always have a love for her, and today confirmed that truth. However, *that* Emma and *that* Drew no longer existed.

As he looked at the massive front porch where they spent many days, his mind drifted to one of the conversations that marked the turning point in their relationship. They had been like a brother and sister until their junior year in high school.

On that crisp, October day, the sky was a deep fall-like blue, and the smell of burning leaves wafted through the air. *"So Drew, do you think there's only one person placed in the world for someone? You know, like everyone has a great love out there somewhere just waiting on them?"*

"What the crap is going on in that crazy head of yours, Em?"

"Believe it or not, we were having this conversation in Ms. Hill's class when the bell rang today. It really made me think, and now I can't get it out of my head. We're starting our poetry section in English, and she was telling us about different passages we could read to get us motivated to write our own stuff."

"Well, we didn't get that far in Mrs. Parks' class. We can't all be brainiacs and be in the 'advanced English' class." He loved to get her stirred up, and making fun of her studious nature always did the trick. Not today, though. She was seriously caught up in her philosophical moment. After throwing a clump of dirt at her, he tried to lay off the jokes and asked, *"Like what kinda stuff were you supposed to read?"*

"You know, the classic romances like Jane Eyre and her

Mr. Rochester, or Elizabeth Bennett and Mr. Darcy. You know, the ones in the literature books they're always pushing on us. Do you believe love like that really exists?" While she spoke, she ate her favorite snack—an apple and peanut butter. Every apple slice had to be covered with peanut butter. She even kept a jar of peanut butter in her book bag just in case she spotted a good apple.

He sat there for a moment and then shook his head. "Yeah, I really do."

"So, do you believe in love at first sight—that true love lasts forever—the 'be still my heart' kind of thing? Do you think you can place a time stamp on the very moment you fall in love? Is there like a certain day it's supposed to happen, or what?"

"I've always felt that I had a soul mate somewhere—if that's what you're asking." He watched her facial expression change, and for the first time, he saw her differently. He saw the beautiful woman she was becoming and not the sixteen-year-old best friend, who happened to be a girl.

"Soul mate, huh? So what's your definition of a 'soul mate'?" She asked, placing her peanut butter jar down while tilting her head to the side. Drew knew that meant she was really listening.

Drew looked away and felt the breeze blowing with a slight nip in the air as twilight fell among the massive oaks that towered above the rooftop. He set his eye on the first star of the night and began his lament that would echo inside the walls of his heart far past that night.

"Well, Em, I think it's like a best friend, but more. I read somewhere once it's like the one person in the world that gets you better than anyone else. You know, like really gets you. Someone that makes you a better person. They don't actually 'make' you be better. They just bring out your good *just because they inspire you to. It has to be someone you can carry with you forever. It's the one person that believed in you and accepted you long before anyone else did or would—the one that knows all your dreams, your secrets, your faults— and still loves you anyway, and no matter what happens, that person will always be your other half."*

In the next breath without hesitation, Emma spoke before she thought. "Kinda like us, huh? Without the love stuff, of course."

The sound of his cell phone jolted him out of his trance. Darby, his fiancée, was calling. He realized he had been at "The Point" too long—physically and mentally. After all, that was all just kid stuff.

Chapter Two

*"The most beautiful discovery that true friends can make
Is that they can grow separately without growing apart."*
~Author Unknown

EMMA TRIED TO compose herself before she entered Ella Ashby's shop. She was so happy to be home again and was more than ready to see her mom. Nothing was better than getting her "Mom Fix." They had always been extremely close since it was just the two of them. Emma's father, Carter Ashby, died when she was eight years old. Emma was a true daddy's girl. He was a professional photographer and taught Emma to see the beauty and magic in everything—making the ordinary extraordinary. He expressed that beauty through pictures, but Emma's passion for expressing beauty came from writing.

He was the love of her mother's life, and soon after they met in college, they were married. After college, they moved to Memphis, TN. He worked as a freelance photographer for various magazines.

Once, while on assignment, he stumbled upon the quaint town of Leyton, snuggly tucked at the foot of the Smokies. It was the perfect place to live the American dream, and when Ella saw it, she loved it as well. They purchased an old store building right on the town square. They worked hard restoring it to its former beauty. Inside, the old brick walls brought authenticity to the place. They knew it was the perfect setting for a photography studio and decided a portion of it would be used to display his photography, as well as other local artists' works.

Carter had traveled to many places during the course of his life because his father was an airline pilot, and had made it a priority to show his son the world. Although that was exciting, when Ella and Carter found out Emma was on the way, all he wanted was to settle down and have security. As a result, "Prints Charming" was established.

When Emma was eight years old, Carter had the chance to travel to Greece with some old college friends for an archeological dig. He called the night before his flight home and could hardly wait to get home to his two girls. He also was anxious to get his film developed and share his adventure with them — and with the town of Leyton. He never got the chance. His plane went down somewhere over the Atlantic, and his body was never recovered.

Ella Ashby loved her husband and agreed to assist him in every part of the business, but that was his dream — *his* passion. After he died, she was devastated. She knew "Prints Charming" would have to close because she could barely take a picture with a Polaroid much less take professional pictures. She talked to the bank about her options on selling the business and building. The president of the bank, James Andrew Dalton, talked her into holding onto the building for a few months. That was when the Daltons and the Ashbys became more like family than friends.

Liza, Andrew Dalton's wife, wanted to open a gift

shop, and everyone knew of Ella's gift for arranging flowers. As fate would have it, within six months, Flower Petals and Gifts was established. As they say, the rest was history.

"Hey, Mom." She heard her voice echo throughout the old building.

"Em." Her mother ran into the room with arms wide open smiling that smile Emma missed so much. All her turmoil from her chance encounter with Drew diminished in the safety of her mom's embrace. "I didn't expect you until later, honey, but since you're here, put this on and help me."

After Emma put the apron on, they caught up—they laughed, reminisced, and shared the details of each other's lives while working on the Dalton order for the next day. Her mom was still single and dated some, but she had never been serious with anyone after Carter. Although she was only forty-five, beautiful, and successful, she always said a man was the last thing she needed. Emma knew the truth—deep down, no one could compare to her daddy.

"Now, catch me up on all the town gossip, Mom. You know all the good stuff, so start at the top."

Her mom shared information about who was having an affair, dealing drugs, and who was bankrupt. This week, it seemed to be all the same person. Her favorite update was about the local church, though. She laughed when she heard about the awful preacher who forgot to turn the television camera off in the sanctuary after the prior Sunday service. The entire town heard him talking about one of his parishioners.

Ever since Emma's friend from school went through a divorce and moved home, the preacher had not said hello to her once. Every Sunday she sat on the front pew in his congregation, and for an entire six months, he never once acknowledged she was there. Yep, he deserved to be exposed for the little weasel he was. They laughed for quite some time over that bit of news.

Mama El, which everyone in town often referred to her as, also reminded Emma that the annual Flywheel Festival was the next day and that her friends from high school all wanted her to come.

The bells on the front door jingled. "Mama El? It's me, Jane."

Turning the corner, Emma squealed, "Jane," ran to her dear friend, and gave her a big hug.

"Em. When did you get in?"

Emma and Jane were extremely close. Jane was actually the best friend Emma had in the world. Her job allowed very little time for socializing, and since she had broken things off with Alec Grisham, she really was relationship challenged.

In the midst of a hug with Jane, Emma saw a very familiar name on the order board above her mom's worktable. Her heart stopped. She felt the energy drain from her body. There, on a piece of white notebook paper, read the words—*Dalton-Spenser Wedding—August 20.*

Jane and Ella were immediately aware of what Emma had seen. For a moment, no one knew exactly what to say. Finally, Ella spoke saying, "Emma, I was going to tell you. It just…"

Jumping in to rescue Mama El, Jane protested, "It just happened. Last week. He just proposed to her last week, if that makes any difference."

"What Jane and I are trying to say is, we really

didn't know how to tell you. We both agreed that this was news to hear face-to-face and not over the phone."

"Your mom is right, honey. Em? You okay?"

Emma could no longer feel her own heart, but the last thing she would do is allow this to shake her—at least not in front of them. That was why she made The Point her first stop in Leyton before she ventured anywhere else. She wanted to make sure she understood reality and could finally put her childhood fantasy to rest.

She responded with a stoic, "Of course I'm fine. Just a little surprised he didn't mention it when I ran into him earlier at the Café, but after all this time, it's not like we are still... well... anything, really. Time sure can change things, can't it?"

She stood up and cleared off the table where scraps had gathered. She was relieved when the subject changed back to the angry little preacher, and while listening she faked her way through the rest of the day as it slowly faded into night. She died inside a little more than she thought possible and was grateful when all was finished for the evening. She hugged her mom and Jane goodnight knowing they were going to have a full-scale conversation about her when she left, but she had to leave—she was falling apart, and she knew she could not hold herself together much longer.

What was wrong with her? They had been teenagers—just kids. Why did this still bother her so much? Would she ever get Drew out of her system, or especially, out of her heart?

Finally, she made her way upstairs. She had never been more thankful than in that moment for her mom converting the second floor of the shop into an apartment after she left for college. When Emma reached her room, she closed the door, her eyes immediately locked on her bulletin board still hanging on her wall. The words were those of Earnest Hemingway from *A Farewell to Arms*, "The world breaks everyone and afterward many are strong in the broken places." *If that were true, I should be steel by now.*

She fought back the tears as she reached for the box under her bed. She had to look for proof that her memories of Drew were real. Her world was so different now. She had grown into a mature, career-oriented woman. The days of the young girl with silly dreams about writing novels with fairy tale endings were long gone. Although she had only been home for a few hours, she could already tell that she was slowly reverting to the seventeen-year-old version of herself. She had once believed in true love. The proof of that, she now held in her hand.

Opening the box was like pulling a blanket of comfort around her. She transported back in time — back into a world she loved and somehow barely recognized. That Emma Ashby dreamed of writing. That Emma would marry the love of her life, her soul mate, but that would not happen. He was engaged to be married to someone else — in August of all months.

She almost laughed aloud when she came across the photos from her sophomore year at LHS. That was the year she was obsessed with anything and everything 80s, although her musical heart never wavered from her true love for the 70s. She looked down at the picture she held in her hand. She read the back, *Halloween 2002 Drew Dalton, Emma Ashby, Jane Stephens, Pearson Straus, Calvin Scott (Moose), and Molly Gordon.* "Now that was a crew," she said to herself as her mind drifted.

"Em, Really? Boy George?"

"Come on, Cindy Lauper couldn't have chosen a better date? Don't hate, Drew, and be still so your hair stays on under your hat. One more bobby pin and then makeup."

"Boy George? Out of the entire 80s genre, you pick Boy George and Cindy Lauper."

"Hey, I love me some Culture Club and Cindy Lauper. Hey, be still. Besides, you're just jealous that Moose is sporting the Michael Bolton mullet and you aren't. Now then, tah dah."

"Em, no make-up please."

"Andrew Dalton. Be still. Just a little. You have no choice."

"Okay, but no lipstick, absolutely none."

"Drew, shout your mouth and pucker up."

"Oh Cindy, Cindy, ooooo baby—thought you'd never ask."

He grabbed her by the waist and tickled her relentlessly until they rolled onto the floor. He played as if he was going to kiss her on the lips when he growled and went for a neck bite instead.

She decided to pack her little box back up and put it back under her bed because these memories were affecting her in some sort of altered sense of reality.

She assured herself as she turned out the light, "Letting go is always best. People change, and life goes on. Besides, if you hold on to yesterday, you miss your tomorrow." Ironically, she really wished she could just skip her actual tomorrow.

She fell asleep singing, "Girls... just want to have fu-un... oh girls just wanna have fun," She vowed to have some fun for old-times' sake. After all, as the great

The Point

Scarlett O'Hara said, "Tomorrow is another day."

Chapter Three

"When you throw dirt, you lose ground."
~Texan Proverb

EMMA STARED AT the invitation on her nightstand before she ever got out of the bed; everything seemed so surreal.

*You are cordially invited to attend a
Private Grand Opening Tour and Dedication
Of
Hastings Hall
Saturday, April 26, 2014
From 10:00 AM-12:00 PM
273 Dalton Drive
Leyton, TN
(Light hors d'oeuvres will be served)*

A good night's sleep did wonders for her demeanor. She had a newfound confidence. She would not only make it through the weekend, but she would actually enjoy it. After all, she would see many of her former classmates, friends, and neighbors.

The Flywheel Festival was a huge deal in Leyton. The entire town showed up, and Dalton Drive was closed to through traffic. Sinclair Hastings Park transformed as out-of-town and local merchants set up booths throughout the area. From The Nut Hut's tasty treats to Barb's Blessings off the square, the hometown businesses represented, as well as those from surrounding counties. The food vendors set up in a makeshift outdoor food court, and between the shopping and food-court area, the parking lot served as the main. A stage was set up by using a flatbed truck. Sound equipment was brought in (compliments of Drew's side business, The Sounding Board), and the entire lot was transformed into a dance floor. Over the years, the festival had grown so that it moved into the street making it a true hometown celebration, often bringing friends and loved ones back home.

Emma knew she should be more excited about reuniting with old friends, but she was not the same person she was years ago. The Emma they remembered was a vivacious, fun-loving, spontaneous girl, full of life and deeply in love with Drew Dalton. This version of herself was someone she was not even accustomed to yet. Now she was more reserved, protected, mature, cautious, serious—boring. The biggest part of her seemed to be missing, which was why the one serious relationship she had in the past didn't work out.

Alec Gresham was in the accounting department at Barlow and Stallings. He was intelligent, with a promising future, and every single woman in Tuscaloosa would have given anything to be seen with him. Soft brown hair, golden-brown eyes, olive skin tone that offset his perfect lips, which framed the amazing smile that could bring a woman to her knees. He was a beautiful man, inside and out, and he was crazy about Emma.

They dated for over two years, but he was not, nor would he ever be, Drew Dalton. After two years, she finally realized the most vital part of her was missing—her heart. She knew no matter how hard she tried or wanted him to fit, Alec could not, nor ever be able to, grow another heart inside of her. When she left Leyton, she also left her heart, and she realized that she couldn't give Alec something she didn't have.

Finally, she showered and made her way downstairs to help her mom. She knew it was time to load up for the reception but dreaded the discussion she knew awaited her. It was too early for the stream of questions headed her way. After pulling her hair up in a ponytail and putting on her Yankees cap, she slipped into a pair of faded jeans and an old LHS shirt then headed down the stairs to help her mom.

Upon reaching the base of the stairs, however, she froze in mid step. She overheard an all-too-familiar voice talking with her mom, and she was not caffeinated enough to deal with it. Having no choice, she took a few deep breaths before walking into the room. Julie Dalton Scott, Drew's sister, stood in the kitchen with a stunningly beautiful brunette at her side. The ladies helped Ella load the ferns Liza wanted to borrow for the day. Emma's breath returned slowly, and after a few breathing exercises, she made her way into their presence.

"Hey, Julie. It's good to see you. How have you been?" Emma asked trying desperately to hide her exploding nerves.

"Well, well, well, if it is not *Miss* Emma Ashby in the flesh. How long has it been now, about seven years?" Julie spoke in a condescending tone. She continued with the same arrogance. "Well where *are* my manners? Emma Ashby, I would like for you to meet Darby Spenser—Drew's fiancée." With a sinister grin, she continued. "Darby, this is Emma, an old friend of Drew's he went to school with."

Although she was astounded by the entire ordeal, she still had enough southern charm and spunk to not allow Julie to get the best of her, especially on her home turf. Instead, Emma answered with poise and grace. She knew it made Julie squirm, and that made Emma very happy. "Well, it is so nice to meet you, Darby. I heard about your engagement. Congratulations. I certainly hope you will be very happy," she stated with a smile.

"It's so nice to finally put a face with your name, Emma. I have heard many wonderful things about you over the years. I hope to see you later today. I know Drew will be glad to see you."

Still holding her own, Emma responded with steel magnolia confidence. "Certainly. I look forward to seeing you both."

Emma glanced at her mom and realized that she consciously had to stop her mouth from dropping open. Emma knew her mom was worried about her so she wanted to hide her inner turmoil as much as possible. Ella loaded the last two ferns in the truck and told Julie that she'd arrive in an hour with the flower arrangements.

Emma waited inside for her mom's return. She had learned to avoid people like Julie Scott. Although Emma never understood Julie, she remembered when Julie seemed nicer. She almost seemed to care the last time they spoke, although it was a day she did not choose to remember often.

Emma was only a little girl when Julie left for

school, so what did she know? She could have always been this way, but Emma sensed Julie's strong dislike of her had grown. It never mattered because out of all the years she spent hanging out at the Daltons', it had just been Drew, his mom, and dad. Having lost her father at such a young age, 'Daddy D,' as Emma referred to him, always seemed to fill that void when possible. He treated her like his daughter right down to his pet name for her. Emma would always be his 'Emmy Em.'

'Drew's Daddy' is actually what Emma called him for a while, but one day, she just started calling him 'Daddy D,' and that is how it remained. 'Emmy Em' is what she called M&M's when she was a little girl, and it always melted Andrew Dalton Sr.'s heart. So, he started calling her 'Emmy Em,' and it stuck.

Drew always joked with his dad that Emma was his favorite child, which probably didn't help Julie's animosity toward her. It never made sense to her why Julie was so mad at her, though. Julie and John had a successful business, and even though she was cold and detached to Emma, she seemed to have a great marriage. She clearly loved her husband and adored their five-year-old son, John Benjamin Scott, Jr., better known as Benji Scott. Emma decided it really didn't matter how Julie felt about her now, because it was very unlikely they would run into each other often. However, for the next few days, it may be extremely difficult running into her again. Before Emma could start talking herself into skipping it all together and heading back to Tuscaloosa, Ella came back inside the shop.

"Emma, I am sorry. I know that must have been

hard. First thing this morning having to deal with that frosty woman, Julie, but then to meet Drew's fiancée in the same moment. Well, I know that must have been tough. Although, I must say, you held up fine, and that scares me just a little." That was an understatement.

Putting on her best front, she responded, "I am fine, Mom. It has been seven years. We were kids. I am fine, really."

"Em, can I ask what exactly happened between you and Drew anyway, *since* you are okay and all. You never really told me, you know."

"That is because there is nothing to tell. I went to Greece for the summer. Then I chose to work for Barlow and Stallings as an intern and go to University of Alabama. We chose different paths, schools, lives. I made my choice, and he made his. That's that."

Her mom remained quiet.

"Mom, really. It's okay," she repeated again hoping to convince herself as well as her mother.

With a faint smile, Ella left her daughter so she could get dressed for the occasion. On the way up the stairs, she reminded herself how Emma was, and she knew when her daughter made her mind up not to talk, she was not going to talk. Although she didn't believe her, she saw a little of the fiery Emma she had once known—the Emma she had seldom seen in the past years. She knew this day was going to be one to remember.

Emma, on the other hand, was furious. To herself, she mulled over the situation. *Really? Do you really want to be this way, Julie? Today of all days?* Although Emma wanted to retaliate, she knew she must take the high road today. Ms. Liza and Daddy D were like family, and Drew—well, no matter what happened, he was still Drew. So, she went upstairs to get ready, and along the way, she rethought her outfit. If she had to take the high road, at least she would look her very best while doing it. Besides, it felt good to know she still had that spunk inside her. "Yes," she said to herself with a smile. "Today is going to be an interesting day. It's good to be home."

Chapter Four

"When your heart is in your dream, no request is too extreme."
~Jiminy Cricket

JANE CAME BY to up pick Emma. She knocked, walked inside, and called out for her. "Emma? Hey, Emma, it's me. Ready?"

"Coming," Emma called as she reached the bottom of the stairs.

"Too, too cute. Love the outfit, perfect."

"Thanks. It's Rebecca Minkoff. I got it last year when we filmed that commercial spot for The Diamond Broker account in North Carolina."

"That was yours? 'A cut above the rest'?"

"Yes, ma'am, it was," Emma said curtly. "Anyway, we have to wear clothes that are versatile today so I'm wearing heels to the reception, and then, voila—flip flops, Tommy Bahama raffia hat, and my Illesteva sunglasses." Emma felt herself coming into her own skin for the first time in years. Home was a good idea.

Jane was cute as always. She was five-foot-three, with auburn hair, and a medium complexion, but she always managed to tan prettier than anyone did. Jane had emerald green eyes and was known to speak her mind often. She also had a dry wit like no other person

Emma had ever known. They worked well together, and when Emma wasn't with Drew, Jane was her gal. Jane dated some in high school, but not much. She was extremely particular, and no one ever measured up. She dated in college, but no one suited her there either. Jane taught school in Louisiana after college, but it was too far from her Tennessee roots for her. So she got a job teaching first grade at Leyton Elementary and moved home.

For now, the ladies were enjoying the single life, and today would certainly be no exception. As they drove up in Jane's vintage BMW, they squealed the tires for old times' sake before getting out of the car.

"Jane, you are rockin' that dress. J Crew is always a great choice—especially black. Black is always the best choice. You are one good-looking lady, if I do say so myself." She gave her friend a wink while reaching for the door.

Wondering what to expect, Emma sighed heavily. She was nervous and excited at the same time, which usually warranted blotches on her chest. That's why she decided to go with a larger necklace. Her dress had a lower cut neckline, and she hoped the piece of jewelry would cover up any redness she might acquire.

Many people attended the dedication. Emma knew some of them, but others she had never seen before. All eyes shifted toward them as they made their way to the champagne fountain. Hearing a familiar voice, Emma was elated.

"Emmy Em."

Emma's eyes lit up as she raced into the arms of Andrew Dalton. "Daddy D. It's so good to see you. I have *missed* you *so much*."

He picked her up as if she were still five years old and twirled her around before placing her feet on the ground with a kiss on the cheek. "How's my girl doing?"

"I'm great," she said still holding his arm in a hug. "And how's my best man?"

"I can't complain." He took her hands and stepped back to admire her once again. "Honey, you look fantastic. It has been too long since I've seen you. Have you seen Liza?"

"Not yet. Where is she?"

Andrew scanned the room until he found her across the room—with Julie. "There she is. She and Julie are over at the podium, probably getting ready for her speech."

If looks could kill a person, Emma was sure the look Julie gave her would put her six feet under. When Liza caught Emma's eye, she dropped everything to come greet her with open arms, which Julie didn't appreciate. She walked away clearly agitated that her dad and mom were still so adoring to Emma after all these years.

"Emma, sweetheart," Liza said. She held her in her arms before patting tears from the corners of her eyes. "Oh, honey—you look amazing." She then she turned around and spoke to Jane. "And hey there, Miss Jane. You are lovely as ever, too. Tell me something. How is it that you two lovely ladies are still single?"

They laughed and shrugged their shoulders. Then Jane threw in a typical dry humor response. "Oh, just lucky, I guess."

While Liza and Emma caught up, Jane went to get a champagne refill. Just as Jane returned with the champagne, Julie returned with Drew and Darby clasped on each of her arms. Emma was grateful that Jane brought her a new glass of champagne as well because she was about to need it.

In an extremely facetious tone, Julie said, "Hello ladies. We meet again."

"Hey." They each responded half-heartedly but with southern charm and politeness, no doubt. The great thing about being a southern lady is that even if you are furious or sad, you can hide it like a professional poker player.

Emma further went on to say with a smile, "Hello to you, too, Drew and Darby. It's so good to see you again, and Drew, I suppose congratulations are in order?" Then she lifted her glass and took a sip.

DREW COULD BARELY look into her eyes. He said a short thanks and took a long sip of his drink. Thankfully, Liza announced it was time for the dedication, so Drew excused himself and made his way to the sound room. He placed his headgear on, praying the throbbing in his chest would calm down enough so that he could concentrate on the moment at hand. It was all he could do not to grab Emma and hold her. What was he thinking? Was he not over this?

He stared at Darby Spenser from the window of the sound room. She was introduced to him at one of the lowest points of his life. He left for college after the breakup with Emma but almost dropped out a time or two. He was depressed and began drinking. He never came home, and everyone that knew him worried that he had taken a dark turn in his life. Everyone was hoping he would meet someone and get his mind off Emma, but at the rate he had been going, no one would want him.

Finally, one weekend when he actually came home, John and Julie came for a visit, and Darby came with them. There was an immediate connection between them, and for the first time in a long, long time, he felt that someone saw him for him and maybe, just maybe, he felt a faint beat of something resembling a heart again. He soon found his smile—and even his personality returned. Darby loved him unconditionally and completely, even in his broken state. She had always been so kind and perfect. Darby helped him out of the darkness his life had become, and for that, he could not help loving her in return. Life had worked out after all, not as he planned, but it was good. He finished school, returned to his former job at the radio station, and was working toward establishing his own business—The Sounding Board.

He also, just recently, approached his family and town council about another project that was long overdue. Maybe that was why it made him so flustered being around Emma again. Maybe he was just apprehensive about the conversation he planned to have with her later that day. There was no way he could do this project without her, and today he planned to ask, or plead rather, for her help.

He jumped when he heard his mom begin her speech. "Excuse me. Excuse me. Could I please have your attention for a moment? First, I would like to thank each of you for coming this morning to the dedication of Hastings Hall. As you know…"

As his mom continued her speech, he glanced again at Darby, his beautiful, sweet Darby. He smiled gently, but it faded as he noticed Emma just beyond her. His mind had yet another flashback. The pain was still so fresh he could almost hear himself crack inside. He closed his eyes, but all he could see were images from the past—his and Emma's past. Performing those silly plays she wrote for them as kids, swimming in the creek after a big rain, discussing life on the porch, teaching her to drive (trying to anyway), football games, Mazi's. He finally opened his eyes hoping it would stop. It stopped all right, but instead of going away, it stopped on one specific memory. He couldn't help smiling as he remembered the first time he took her in his arms and kissed her.

"Okay, Miss Know-it-All about music. I have a Queen song that I happen to know you have never heard."

"Yeah, right. You know I know my seventies music." She spoke with hand to her heart. "Especially the all-time great Freddie Mercury. Don't even play."

"No Em, I am serious. Listen." He turned off the engine and they sat in silence waiting for the music to begin. The sun settled behind the western sky as the orange and purple colors lent the perfect backdrop for the moment.

In the cool of the early evening just as the first stars began to break through the sky, Emma and Drew sat, and for the first time, Emma heard the song, "Love of My Life."

"Drew, this is beautiful. Is that a harp? I can't believe I never…"

"Shhh, Em. Just listen…"

He tried to keep his feelings in check, but with every note, he knew there was no use fighting it any longer. He loved so many little things about her, including her deep passion for music. Her beauty simply captivated him in a way nothing ever had. As the sun completely gave way into night, he felt his heart 'give way' as well. In that moment, he knew in his heart he was completely, and totally, in love with her. Emma now possessed him— body and soul. He thought he always knew it, but he had not known the depth of her effect on him until that moment. Their eyes met just as the song ended. As soft as he possibly could, he asked, "Do you feel it?"

Shaking her head yes, a single tear stained her young cheek. Breathlessly, she answered, "Yes."

"This is it, Em. This is the magic. This is real." He paused briefly before confessing a bit hesitantly, "I... I love you... I think I always have." He could barely speak through his own tears stuck in his throat.

"I love you too, Drew, I love you."

Then, in that moment, under the soft, fresh, moonlit night, Drew kissed Emma, his Emma, for the very first time. Tenderly and so softly, he kissed the tear from her cheek while brushing her face with his thumb. Then he placed a loose strand of hair behind her ear and leaned into her. With all his love and all his heart, he kissed her soft lips. The mere touch seemed to rivet through each of their bodies. It seemed as if every moment of their lives led them to this.

Suddenly, the applause jolted him back into the present, and he realized his mom's speech was over. He was thankful for the solitude because he felt Emma dancing in his eyes; he didn't want Darby, or anyone else, to see that.

He forced himself to shake the gripping trance by thinking back to that August night—the night that it all ended. Ironically, it ended at the same place they began—at The Point. With the stern reminder of how they ended and the choices made, he came back to his reality, walked out of the booth, and out of his memories.

Chapter Five

"She's strong enough to walk away, but broken enough to look back."
~Author Unknown

EMMA AND JANE excused themselves to change clothes. Once they had successfully gone from dressy to casual daywear, they went back to say good-bye to the Dalton family. After Emma promised not to leave without coming by the house for a visit, they finally headed out the door—that is, until Drew called Emma's name.

"Emma. Hey… Em, wait up a minute."

Her heart could barely take him calling her Em again. She turned around and looked at him.

"Hey, can we talk for a minute? I really need—"

She suddenly cut him off. "Drew."

Jane suddenly interrupted, telling Emma that she was going over to the festival and that she'd meet her there. From the looks of it, Jane thought this could take a while. Emma nodded reluctantly to her friend and continued speaking to Drew.

"It has been great seeing you again, Drew. Really. But there is really nothing—"

Drew interrupted, "No, no you don't understand. That's not what I want to talk about. Look, Emma, what we had…is our past. Can't we *at least* be friends?"

A little embarrassed, she shook her head and softly replied, "Yes."

Exhaling a sigh of apprehension, Drew asked again a little more earnestly, "So, got a minute?"

"*Just* a minute," she said as he opened the door for her and they walked out the backdoor to the outdoor courtyard. She had seen it earlier while on the tour, but it still took her breath for a second time. The fountains made the garden one of such tranquility, elegance, and beauty.

Drew paused to look at Emma standing in the garden. For just a second, his eyes almost gave him away until he heard Darby and Benji calling for Uncle Drew. He leaned inside the door and motioned for them to come outside.

Benji loved his Uncle Drew. He came up every other weekend with his mom, dad, and Darby to work on the new store they were opening downtown. Julie could not wait to be a chain, as she referred, but all Benji Scott cared about was hanging with his uncle.

"Uncle Drew, come with me to the festival. Please, please, please. I'll let you bench press me later."

Drew laughed and said, "Come here, buddy. I want you to meet a special friend of mine. Her name is Emma. Emma, this is the one and only Benji Scott."

"Glad to meet you, Benji Scott." Emma shook his hand.

"You're hot!" Benji exclaimed loudly, trying to make his young eyebrows move up and down while attempting to wink.

"Benji," Drew exclaimed, completely taken back by his nephew's statement.

"Well, she is, don't you think?"

THE *Point*

After an awkward moment that seemed like forever, they all nervously laughed, and Drew bent down and looked into Benji's eyes.

"Tell you what—I promise I will meet you at the festival soon, but first I need to discuss something with my friend, Emma. How about we meet for ice cream later? Deal?"

"Deal," he yelled as he ran away.

Darby followed behind and waved good-bye until Drew stopped her.

"Darby, please stay. This is our project, so we both should plead our case. Besides, this lady is a tough one, and I need all the help I can get." He laughed and gave Emma a wink as if they truly were just two old friends.

It was all too strange for Emma, but she was relieved when Darby agreed to stay. She was also glad to see him smile and relax a little. She saw the Drew she remembered—the Drew she knew—the Drew she loved. He looked happy, and for that, she was grateful, in a strange way. Happy looked good on him, but then again, almost everything looked good on him.

At Drew's leading, the three of them walked along a cobblestone sidewalk with a beautiful and fragrant landscape sprinkled along the way. She was amazed at the ground's beauty. Seeing and smelling lavender, rosemary, and lemon verbena was heavenly. She also recognized a few night blooming flowers mixed in among the greenery. It was quite exquisite and such a contrast from anything she'd ever seen in the small town before.

"Drew, this is amazing. I can barely take it all in. You all must be thrilled with this place. Leyton has needed something like this for years. Just think of the events that will take place here. I absolutely love it."

"We're going to be married right in this very garden in August, evening of course, so it will be tolerable," sweet Darby said with a sincere smile.

Emma wondered how in this world Darby had ever become friends with that monster of a lady, Julie. Emma was certain Darby didn't realize how close she and Drew had been. There was no way she could possibly be as comfortable as she seemed walking along with them if she had. Trying to keep up her appearance, Emma responded to the news keeping up her façade of southern charm.

"How lovely I am sure that will be. I know you two will be very happy."

Clearing his throat, Drew stopped for a moment, stepped into a building, and came out driving a golf cart. Darby insisted Emma sit up front with Drew. They all climbed onto the cart, and Drew drove forward until stopping at the top of a grassy hill overlooking the span of the grounds.

Emma's mouth gaped open while her mind tried to process all that she saw. Astonished by the beauty before her, tears crept into her eyes as a spontaneous result. She quickly became aware of herself and forced them back while maintaining her smile.

"Drew, I cannot believe it. You actually did it." Her eyes spoke with wonder. "It's... it's..."

He finished her sentence, "It's *our* world, Em. Just like we dreamed it would be when we were just two bratty kids... lost in our daydreams."

Emma was acutely aware of the way Drew was looking at her. It felt as if he were soaking in all that her eyes could see. She couldn't help getting lost for a moment with him the way she had always done.

She finally spoke while still surveying the land, "True beauty like this can't be created you know," she said lost in her own thoughts. "This kind of beauty just *is*."

As she continued to look out into the beyond, Drew's eyes simply rested on her, and he added in a hush, "I couldn't agree more."

Finally Darby spoke up. "It really is lovely here."

Emma was aware that Darby had been watching them. Was she aware of their past? Did she recognize their connection? It didn't really matter because she was lost to Drew in the moment. Thankfully, a bee buzzed past Darby, causing her to squeal and breaking the awkwardness between them.

As Emma put on her sunglasses, she had never been more thankful she was a woman who firmly believed in accessorizing on every occasion because at this moment, her sunglasses were her new best friend. Her eyes were glassing over, and it was all she could do to keep tears from spilling over her lids. Now she prayed her nose didn't betray her by turning red.

However, when they stopped and got out of the cart at the footbridge, a tear she could not stop fell down her cheek. She almost melted when Drew, took his thumb and brushed her face allowing his hand, not to mention his eyes, to linger a bit too long after she removed her glasses. Emma gave him an appreciative, yet confusing look before putting them back on. Thankfully, Darby was not with them yet, but shortly, she was back at Drew's side.

Emma could hardly believe it. Everything was just as they always planned. Drew had even used the detailed, decorative wood from the old shed behind the cookhouse at the mansion to build the footbridge. She wanted so badly to look underneath the hand railing to see if he used the piece they carved their initials in, but not only did she realize how ridiculous she would look, she was certain that this was his new life and the old was gone. Of course, he hadn't even remembered that wood.

"Darby, this is how Emma and I spent our childhood. We played just about everything you can imagine on the land between the Hall and The Point. Hey, Em," he said lightly touching the top of her shoulder and turning her attention beyond the bridge. "This walkway leads straight to The Point, but look around—the apple orchard is south of the land, and there is a grove of Pecan trees in the northern part. There also is a walking track all along the perimeter of the land complete with swings and benches throughout as well, but the lake and land included with the main house is private. Hey, I even built a small cabin beside the lake—and a new dock. When we drive back, I'll drive you by way of the lake, but you *really* need to see it at sunset. You know there is nothing more beautiful that watching the sunset on this land."

She knew what he was doing. He had to remember the night of their first kiss as well as she did, and deep down, she knew he added that comment so it would cross her mind. Not to mention the other hundreds of times they had been caught up in their passion all over this land. Some of her most tender moments had been sharing those sunsets with him, but he didn't want her anymore. He had made his choice. Part of him, she thought, just wanted to torment her.

THE *Point*

Emma was right. Drew was pulling out all the stops trying to hurt her; yet at the same time, he seemed to want to hold her so close he could hear her heartbeat. The longer he was near Emma, the harder it was to keep those buried feelings at bay. He needed to stay in the present with Darby. He loved Darby. They were getting married. He loved Darby. Right?

Finally Emma spoke. "I love the variety of daylily colors and the tons of yellow daffodils scattered around everywhere. It is really *our* dream. Our imaginary world has *actually* come to life." She looked out and could almost see her young self with a crown of flowers on her head as she danced with arms flying at her side amongst them. How nice it would be to feel that kind of happiness, joy, and freedom again.

"Well, that was in the dream, Em, remember? The yellow flowers, daylilies, all of it. The community loves this place, 'The Grove.' We actually haven't decided on a name yet, but the town is calling it that for now, it seems. I like that it gives the entire town and surrounding area a place to come with their families or to come for a quick escape to an imaginary place—a place you can feel and see magic."

"You're right, Drew. It is perfect, just as we imagined." Although she knew that was not the only dream she and Drew had, it dawned on her as to why she may be there. Then the words actually came from Drew's mouth, leaving her emotionally paralyzed.

"Emma, we, Darby and I, well, we want to refurbish the old mansion, The Point. We have done everything to this plot of land my great-great grandfather left my family, but now, it's time we complete it. Darby will be moving here to open the new store in July, but she is so busy between the store finalities and the wedding, she has limited time. Actually, she has none." While now standing at Darby's side, he reached for her hand, pressed his lips against it, and smiled at her, leaving Emma with a stabbing pain in her heart.

Emma forced herself to breathe and desperately hoped that they could not see her oncoming panic attack. *Breathe, breathe, breathe,* she said to herself. She could not believe this was happening.

Then Darby finally joined in. "Besides, Emma, if this... all this beauty came from your imagination, I cannot fathom the plans you must have swarming around inside you for the mansion. Your love for the place is evident. Your heart shows up good here, ya know? We need you."

"I don't know, Darby," she said while thinking, *Lady, you have no idea how my soul is intertwined in the place or you would never, in a million years, be asking me to help you.*

No sooner did that thought settle inside her than Darby began to speak again. "Emma, you grew up here. You were a huge part of the development of this enchanted place whether you knew it then or even choose to believe it now. I know you are the other half of the dreams Drew has for the mansion, and you can deny it all you want, but that doesn't make it any less true." As Darby finished her plea, she looked at Drew and smiled.

Emma stood there having a complete breakdown inside. *Is this lady for real? How could any human, red-blooded woman not think all of this is odd? She really is clueless or the most understanding person I have ever met.*

They stood for what seemed like an eternity, and

then Emma spoke up. "I appreciate you two having shared this with me and for knowing how much it meant to me, *but* in saying that, I am swamped at work. I am two weeks away from closing on an international ad campaign, and then, well, I really do thank you for the ego boost and for believing I have anything to contribute."

"Will you, Em? Please—for me? For us?" Drew paused a minute before asking, "Will you at least *think* about it? You don't have to answer today or even this weekend. What do you say?"

"Please, Emma. Drew doesn't think he can possibly do this without you. It would mean so much to both of us," Darby said with a slight pout from her bottom lip.

With a deep sigh Emma answered, "Okay, okay. I will think about it." They all smiled, and then Emma added with a jagged glance, "Drew, you better be glad you brought Darby because I have had plenty of practice telling you no."

"Great, then why don't we head back and get to that festival before Benji sends Deputy 'Moose' out looking for me," Drew said and laughed.

"I cannot believe he is policeman—a deputy at that. Well, we don't want to be on his bad side now, do we? Let's scoot," Emma said with great relief.

Chapter Six

*"I always knew looking back on tears would make me laugh,
But I never knew looking back on the laughter would make me cry."
~Author Unknown*

EMMA WAS ELATED to see Ms. Mazi still at the Hall cleaning from her catering job. Emma decided to stay and help her, and when they were done, she rode back to the shop with her to help unload. She was relieved for the sudden change of venue because she suddenly thought the festival was more than she could endure. Emma phoned Jane with her change of plans and promised to meet at the shop later.

Finally, she had some time alone to think about the morning. As she sat out on the front porch of the florist shop, she felt an impending panic attack. What just happened? She knew she had plenty of vacation time, but did she really want to do this? Of course not. Could she even endure this kind of pain—the agony it would cause for the duration of time to complete this project? And how was Julie going to react when she heard about all this? And what about Julie? What was her problem anyway? She clearly had issues, but what had Emma ever done to her? This was too much. She had forgotten how awful small town drama could be. Although, it was tempting to say yes on the spot just to watch Julie completely go off the deep end, but that kind of pain was not worth the pleasure.

Emma was glad to see her mom was back when she finally walked through the door. She knew her Mom would keep her busy, and hopefully she wouldn't have to think about Drew.

"Hey, Mom. I'm home."

"Oh, hey there, you shady lady. Wondered where you had gotten off to. Grab anything—you know the routine," her mom said playfully.

"Everything looked beautiful today, and I love that building. It was also so good to see Mrs. Liza and Daddy D, too. I have really missed them."

"I really thought everything went exceptionally well," Ella remarked. " So, what do you think of Darby?"

"Mom, really? You are absolutely incorrigible," she playfully chided. "Do we have to go there now? I am practically brain dead from the tour of the newest addition to Dalton Acres—or whatever it's going to be called—The Grove, maybe. After a while, everything became a blur."

Ella walked over to her daughter who sat on the bar stool pilfering through scraps of ribbon left on the table. Standing behind her, she kissed Emma on the top of her head. "Emma, ever since you were a little girl you have protected yourself from pain. The only one you ever really let inside your heart in times of great pain was Drew. I remember when you were a little girl and your father died, you went missing," she continued as tears formed. "The entire town was on alert, and Liza called, and said Drew thought he knew where you may be. Sure enough, he was right. We found you at the old Hasting place. Even then, he knew how you loved that place, and even at that young age, he knew you well enough to know where you would go to hide in your darkest moment. He could always find you, reach you, be there for you, rescue you, or whatever you needed him to be, but honey, he is about to marry someone else now. He was your first love—your very *best* childhood friend. It's not healthy to keep all the emotion you must feel inside."

Emma remained stoic and silent. Did her mother not know she knew all these things? Did she not know her heart was breaking because this was supposed to be her life? She remained outwardly calm and remained intact.

Patting her daughter on the back Ella then said, "Well, if you need me, you know I am here. I love you, sweetheart, with all my heart. Please know that." Then as she was leaving the room, she paused in the doorway and said, "It's good to have you home, kiddo. I sure have missed you."

Emma sat there for a minute and suddenly remembered that she better get ready for the big dance at the Flywheel Festival. The festival had become one of the highlights of the year. The live bands performed all day, and then the night would end with the big dance. Much to Emma's delight, the theme for the dance this year was the seventies. It was free to the public with the understanding of dressing according to the genre.

About the time she was deciding what to wear, a knock came at the door. Jane entered dressed in bell-bottoms, a tie-dyed shirt, and flip-flops. She and Jane managed to come up with a last minute seventies look for Emma: a Lynyrd Skynyrd t-shirt, cutoff jeans, and Converse tennis shoes. Of course, accessories were necessary, which included large hoop earrings and a mood ring. Emma was not a fan of the clothing style during that decade, but had always been a fan of the music. Her nervous excitement returned, which frightened her because of the last engagement she experienced with Jane earlier that day.

"Let's take my Jeep. That okay?" Emma asked as she put a final coat of blue glitter fingernail polish on her nails. She also found a thick, leather bracelet with her name embossed in it at the bottom of her junk jewelry box with a peace sign etched in it. She placed it on her wrist, looked at Jane, and said, "I'm ready."

Jane suggested they follow one another in separate cars in case one wanted to leave early. Emma thought the idea was a good one after the day she'd had.

EMMA WAS THRILLED to catch up with her old school friends who were home for the festivities. Old school teachers, classmates, and neighbors arrived, making it seem as if the entire city was out for a night on the town. Everyone wanted to catch up and hear about her life. It felt good to be home, and she found the longer she was there, she found pieces of herself she had forgotten.

She walked over to a booth and bought herself a large unsweetened tea—with extra ice, and then she and Jane found a nice table by the stage. About that time, she heard some familiar voices.

"Emma Ashby. It is so great to see you."

Emma was startled hearing someone scream, but soon a smile crept over her face as she jumped to her feet to hug her former classmate and friend.

"Molly Gordon. Hey. It's so great to see you."

"Molly Gordon Straus, thank you," she said as she pulled back from her friend and gave her a good look over. "Emma, you look fantastic, but I will admit, it scares me a little seeing you and Jane together again," she said with a soft laugh. "Do you remember the night Jane decided she wanted to put a goat into the high school and the two of you searched all over the town of Leyton until you finally found one?"

"Yes, I do. Jane, you crazy nut. Didn't you realize the goat would scratch us to pieces? What in this world made us think we could handle a goat?" Emma asked, playfully jabbing Jane in her side.

As they continued the conversation, they laughed so abruptly and often that people thought they were drunk. About that time, Pearson walked up with Deputy Calvin Scott saying, "I believe there is a warrant for your arrest for stealing old man Norman's goat, Miss Emma Ashby."

"Moose. Pearson Straus." After giving the guys hugs, she stepped back and laughingly joked, "Hey, is it against the law to call you Moose, Mr. Deputy? I can't tell you how great it is to see you guys—all of you. Even if you are rockin' an afro, Pearson."

Molly chimed in, "Hey, that was all his idea to go with the Don King hair." She winked at them all.

An hour later, a few more former classmates joined the group, including Drew and Darby.

"Well, well, you guys are a sight," Drew said reaching his hand out to shake Pearson's hand and giving Molly a hug.

Naturally, all eyes gravitated toward Emma when

he introduced Darby as his fiancée. Then, with her consistent poise and charm, Emma made them all feel at ease as she spoke. "Darby, it's so good to see you again. Get over here with the ladies, or the boys will fill your head full of tall tales."

They all warmed up to Darby, and everyone seemed more relaxed—especially when the music cranked up. Emma was determined to sit out the dance part of the evening. It was one thing to reminisce of the 'days gone by,' but to act like she did in the past was a little much. That was another lifetime ago; she was not that person anymore. "YMCA. Everybody, get on your feet," the DJ from the local station announced. He was a friend of Drew's and had agreed to be the emcee for the night.

Even if she thought she had a choice of not dancing, she was wrong. Her old crew grabbed her hands, and before she knew it, the parking lot-turned dance floor was hopping with arms flying in the air. They could be heard all over town as the roar of the crowd soared in the nighttime air. "Y-M-C-A. It's fun to stay at the Y-M-C-A."

The laughter and fun continued, and Darby was right in the middle of them. Emma genuinely liked her even though she was everything that Emma was not. Darby was kind and quiet. She always seemed to go along with everything Drew did or said, but not in a pathetic, clingy way, just in a truly loving, nice person way. Emma was defiant, hardheaded, argumentative, and loud when she needed to be. Emma assumed she wasn't Drew's type after all.

Emma thought one dance would suffice her friends until "Dancing in the Moonlight" came on and a man that she could not resist asked for a dance. "There's my girl. Dance with me, my Emmy Em," Andrew Dalton said. She knew he was not taking no for an answer anyway.

"Daddy D," she said smiling as she reached out her hands to accept his offer.

They had the most fun of anyone on the floor—dipping and spinning. They even cleared the dance floor when they danced to "Staying Alive." After that, Daddy D had to go sit the rest of the night out with Mrs. Liza.

The tunes continued with KC and the Sunshine Band, the Doobie Brothers, Billy Joel, Gladys Knight, and Abba. Emma could not remember the last time she genuinely laughed and had that much fun. She really had needed this badly. *This night was a good idea after all,* she thought to herself. When they all finally took a break, they ordered drinks from the Tipsy Cow.

"So Emma, you wrote the song for that bug spray commercial?" Molly asked.

"That was you?" Darby asked.

"Guilty," she said as she took a sip from her fruity drink.

"Yes, and the catch phrase: 'Death of bugs is only one spray away'," she added, rolling her eyes while smiling because she knew just how cheesy it sounded. It paid good money though, and that was all that mattered. Right? Why was she suddenly second-guessing her entire life? She kept saying over and over to herself, *"One weekend. One weekend and I'm gone."*

They all laughed and sang the little song.

"So, what is the coolest location you ever got to shoot on?"

"Hands down, that would be Scotland. We

filmed promo shots for a series that was filmed in the Highlands but will air in the States. It is breathtakingly beautiful. Cold, but amazing. We actually stayed a few extra days to tour the country and even stayed one night in a real castle."

"Really?" Molly asked. "I always thought it looked rather dull to me."

Then Jane asked, "What do men really wear under those kilts?"

"I hate to disappoint you, Jane, but I cannot honestly answer that, but you have not lived until you have seen a well-built man in full clan attire," she said with a wink.

"So, speaking of men, are you dating anyone?" Molly's question piqued the attention of the guys at the other end of the picnic table as well.

Taking another sip of her drink, she said, "I dated someone for a few years, Alec Gresham. Great guy, but we are better off as friends. We are the best of friends, actually. If all goes according to plan in a few months, he and I are actually going on an all-expense paid trip to the World Series this year. A company I've been working with has extra tickets, and they offered to even fly us in their private jet. He is the best, and he's practically the only friend I have in Alabama."

"Ask her if he's good looking," Jane chimed in as she walked up with an armload of LHS jerseys she'd borrowed from the school, piling them on the table where Drew sat while informing the crew to put them on.

Smiling at Jane, Emma grinned sheepishly and said, "Yes, very, but some things are just not meant to be."

Drew looked at Jane and said, "Yes ma'am. Damn,

you are bossy as ever."

Emma watched him closely. Was he glad she was single? It looked as if he flinched a little at her statement, but it was probably nothing. She did notice him looking at her, but he quickly turned away when she met his eyes. She wondered if anyone else had noticed anything off with him, or was it just her?

Then conversation continued to progress and after some time it all became about babies. Knowing nothing about being married and much less about motherhood, Emma looked over to Jane to find her friend missing. She walked over to get another drink, and Jane appeared with armload of something.

Emma followed her friend as they rejoined the others asking, "Where the heck have you been, Jane? I've been looking for you."

Emma and Molly helped retrieve some of the items Jane was holding in her arms.

"So, where *have* you been, Jane?" Emma asked again suspiciously.

"Oh, have I got a surprise for you guys." She handed them all Comet jerseys with a squeal.

"Well thanks," Pearson said, "but—"

The familiar tune was now playing in the background to persuade the crowd to join in cheering the former classmates to the stage. Emma and Drew locked eyes and laughed thinking about all the work they put into on that video all those years before. The former classmates gathered their props and made their way up front and center. As the emcee announced the class of 2004, Emma took one last large gulp from her cup and took her place in the middle of the group with a headset microphone that Drew placed on her.

THE *Point*

"Really?" she asked. "Okay, you guys get into your places." Emma nodded for the music to begin again. The old excitement of fun days gone by returned as Elton John sporadically played the intro chords to "Benny and the Jets," or better known in that moment as "We will beat the Jets."

Singing to a music track, without the assistance of Sir Elton unfortunately, they all joined Emma in the song.

Hey you, put your hands together
Comets coming through and we always stick together,
You can try but you will not—bring us down
This is what we'll do
If you're with us, say it loud
"WE—WILL—BEAT—THE—JETS"

After the cheer-song ended and they mingled off the stage area, they all remained on the dance floor for the next song because it was the classic, "Sweet Home Alabama."

Drew made his way to Emma while Moose danced with Darby. "Look at you, you little hypocrite, you."

"Excuse me?" she shot back at him with only a look Emma could give.

"Not *only* are you wearing a Skynard shirt, you are dancing to the song you refused to let me listen to in *my own* car."

"Hey, I live in Tuscaloosa, Alabama, you idiot. What do you expect? Besides, I have come a long way in seven years." She laughed and continued to dance. She was so glad they all were together, and hopefully she could leave the next day with a good memory, having finally put the past behind her.

When the song was done, they all sat down again.

A series of Bee Gee favorites played in the background as they continued catching up with each other's lives. Then, a song played over the speaker that changed the entire dynamic of the evening—for Emma anyway.

Although not as familiar to everyone else, she immediately knew what song was playing. The simple piano chords began and then the harp — that blasted harp and then the words. "Love of my life... you've hurt me, broken my heart... bring it back..." As the song continued, she vaguely heard Darby ask the name of the song.

Without realizing it, Emma replied while staring into nowhere, "*Love of my Life*, by Queen."

When it was over, a melancholy settled over Emma, and her heart filled with the familiar soul-ache she had known for such a long time. She had to get out of there. She had to get out now.

"I have got to get home and pack. Tomorrow will come early."

"Aww, party pooper," someone in the group said, but everyone understood.

Drew merely nodded, stood, and said, "I'll catch up with you later about the offer."

Knowing her answer was a big fat no, she just pretended it was still up in the air to avoid staying any longer. "Well, goodbye, Darby. It was so good to meet you." Hesitantly, she said, "Take care of Drew, okay?" Then with a nod to Drew and hugs for them, she left.
Finally, Emma made her way to her Jeep, and for the first time since her arrival in Leyton, she broke down. She told herself there was no more pretending. The world she had once known was somewhere lost in time, so where did that leave her?

The Point

DARBY EXCUSED HERSELF to the restroom to "freshen up." As Drew watched her walk away, he thought back to the night's events. Although he wanted to dwell on his thoughts of Emma, he knew it was just a memory and nothing more. They were over. He was torn and confused by the emotions he had experienced all night. Emma and Darby being there together was almost more than he could handle. Part of him was relieved Emma was leaving but another part of him was afraid she would refuse his offer and never come back. If he loved Darby, why did that matter so much to him? He was afraid to answer that question so he decided to leave it right where he had kept it over the past years. In the past.

Chapter Seven

"Tears are the safety valve of the heart when too much Pressure is laid on it."
~Albert Smith

EMMA PARKED HER Jeep in front of the florist in an attempt to stop her head from spinning. For a minute, she thought she was going to be sick. How could her heart still hurt this badly—after seven years away from him? She thought she had finally let go of her past. Maybe she'd just been running from it instead. While sitting lost in her thoughts, a rap at the window nearly caused her heart to fail.

"Emma," Jane said tapping the window. "Hey. Get out of there, and let's go inside. It's getting cool out here."

"Jane, you nearly scared me half to death!" Emma exclaimed with a jolt. "I'm tired and just want to go upstairs, soak in a hot tub, go to bed, and forget the entire day even happened."

However, Jane was insistent. "No, not tonight. You are talking to me, Emma Elizabeth Ashby. Even if I have to stay up all night pulling the words out of you, you will talk to me."

"Fine. Have it your way. Come in, and I'll make some coffee."

"Hey, why don't we grab a cup at Mazi's? She's still

open for another hour."

"Whatever. Come on, you bully." She gave her friend an exhausted smile.

They walked down the sidewalk to the café. As they made their way to the table with coffee in hand and feeling a little more at ease, the gang from the Flywheel came in.

"Great. Gee, thanks, Jane. Just what I wanted—more Drew and Darby love."

"Sorry," Jane mouthed quietly as they approached the table and proceeded to join them.

"Seems we keep running into each other everywhere we go today," Darby said with a slight giggle.

Again, Emma wondered just how clueless one person could possibly be. Had she meant so little to him that he had failed to even mention their relationship beyond they were 'good friends'? This was getting old really quick, and tomorrow couldn't come soon enough.

"Small town," Emma said half-heartedly.

"So Jane, what are you up to these days?" Pearson asked.

Emma wondered how they possibly had not covered everything there was to know about one another already. She pretended to listen as Jane proceeded to tell him all about her students, and as she talked, Emma plotted her next move on how to escape. She would go home, pack, and leave first thing tomorrow. She was cold, so she thought she'd try using the fact she was in a T-shirt and cutoff jeans as a plan for escape.

"Look, it's been a blast seeing you all, but again, I must say good night. I am actually freezing and have to get packed,"

Of course the ever so valiant Drew said, "Hang on, Em. Let me run up to my room. I've got just what you need."

Oh my word, he lives upstairs. Would this nightmare ever end? She thought he said he had a cabin on the lake. He lives next door in a room above Mazi's and no one bothered to tell her. Oh wow.

Emma was out of ideas on how to leave and dreading what Drew would come downstairs with. When he returned, she could not believe it. His Yankee sweatshirt. *Great. That will make the heartache go away,* she thought to herself. *Put on his sweatshirt.* She listened to them talk in the background while she tried again to think of the next excuse to leave.

"Here you go, Em." He threw it across the table, looking knowingly at her.

Putting the Yankees sweatshirt on reminded her about her and Alec's plans to see the World Series and that was something good to think about now. Yes, she would think of the fun she and Alec would have. She tried to think of anything other than Drew's shirt that smelled like him—not to mention that she was the reason he had gotten it to begin with. He refused to support any team not born and bred in the South.

"I will have Mom wash and return it next week. Thanks."

"You can keep it. I never wear it, and besides, you are the only reason I bought it in the first place, remember? You know, you were the only goofy person I know in these southern parts that is even a Yankee fan," he said jokingly.

So much for discretion there, Drew, she thought to herself.

Emma had been quiet since the sweatshirt exchange. Molly actually pulled her back into the conversation with a music question before she could plan her next escape.

"Okay Emma, after you left tonight, they played the song 'Without You.' Who had the *better* version— Harry Nilsson or Mariah Carey?" she asked sternly, looking at Drew.

As Emma began to speak, Drew did too. Then, as if it were planned, they said at the same time said, 'Harry Nilsson.'

"Hello? Did she ask you or me?" Emma smarted back at him.

"I knew your answer," he said throwing straw paper at her from across the table.

"She still asked me, not you," she snapped playfully again.

"Do you want me to explain why she likes Harry's better, Molly?" He smiled at Emma as he asked and continued saying, "Because I can tell you exactly why."

"I would love to hear," Molly said, thoroughly entertained and holding her coffee cup for a refill.

"First of all, most of the time, the original is the best. Then, the strings play chords that contrast as they play against the horns as they fade out at the end of the song, but most importantly, Mariah sounds like she has a lisp. Am I right, Em?"

Everyone laughed, including Emma as she begrudgingly admitted that he was right. "Yes, you smart aleck and Molly, Drew will be answering all my questions for the rest of the night."

"Okay. What is the song on the radio now?" Pearson asked Drew.

"'I'd Really Love to See You Tonight'," he answered.

Emma threw in instinctively, "By England Dan and John Ford Coley." They did a quick high five like they were teammates of some imaginary musical team.

"Have you two always been like this about music?" Darby asked. "And Emma, how do you know all this seventies music anyway? You haven't missed one all night."

"Well Darby, my dad died when I was eight years old in a plane crash. He loved music, grew up in the seventies, *and* just happened to have an amazing album collection, so that is how I know so much about it. But, I love the music because it was the greatest decade of music of all time."

"I do not agree with her though," Drew chimed in. "I am more of an eighties guy myself. I have quite a collection." He laughed and jabbed Emma on the shoulder from across the table –clearly still channeling the junior high version of himself.

"Oh no. Here we go again," Jane said with an exaggerated eye roll. "Darby, they had their own special ongoing version of 'battle of the bands' every time music was discussed. Next thing they will start guessing the other one's favorite part of the song," Jane said while Emma shot her a look of disdain.

"No thank you. I can't handle any more coffee," Emma said as the waitress came to make her last rounds. "Could you please get me a…"

On impulse, Drew said, "A large unsweetened tea with extra ice—sorry."

Looking back at Emma he asked, "Are you sure you are from the south? Who drinks unsweetened tea *and* is a Yankee fan in this part of the world anyway?"

It was obvious Drew made that comment as a distraction but the conversation continued to flow.

"But this is the amazing thing, Darby. Watch this." Molly insisted they show their most interesting quirk. "Wonder if you can still do it?" she asked as she cleared the table.

"I don't know, Molly. It's been years, and it's late. Besides, she doesn't want to," Emma started to say, looking sternly at Jane until Darby interrupted her saying in a distinct and purposeful tone, "Yes. I *want* to see it, please."

Emma looked at Drew to see if he was up for it.

He sat directly across the table from her smiling as he said, "Bring it on."

"Okay. Fine," she said with that challenging look.

Then he followed with his game face on saying the same. "Fine."

Each switched almost immediately to their all too familiar competitive mode and got comfortable because they knew this could take some time.

"Okay, lady. Do your thing and see if he can still do his," Jane said as she handed Emma her iPod.

"Now, it's been years since we have even seen each other, so don't expect this to still work," she said. She took Jane's iPod until she looked up and commented, "If Jane has anything anyone even knows on here." Finally she found one she wanted to play. She took a sheet of paper out, wrote her very favorite part down, placed it face down on the table, and pressed PLAY.

"First up, 'A Thousand Years' by Christiana Perri," Molly announced.

As Drew listened, he smiled showing that he knew this from the first chord. "The strings, as the music is softening at the end of the song and builds—especially at the very end, but your favorite part is at the very beginning when you hear the cello for the first time."

Opening the paper it read, "The strings. Particularly as builds—cello my favorite."

"Amazing. After all this time, you can *still* do that." Emma was astonished. "But see if you can do it again."

Again, she wrote out on the paper her favorite part of the song she had chosen thinking there was no way he would ever get this because it was so random. "Second song of the night—'Enchanted' by Taylor Swift," Molly continued.

They all listened to Miss Swift, and at the end of her song, Drew once again commented with a knowing smile.

"Too easy," he said. "She is floored that this young lady can write such songs at her age. It's the words and her gift of writing that Em loves. "

Again, the answer was correct. This infuriated Emma that he still knew her like that. She was hoping he no longer had that connection because it would be much easier to walk away for good.

"Okay, one more, Emma. Please," they all begged—except for Darby.

"Fine. Then I am going home to bed. Besides, they need to close the shop." She laughed but added, "This one will be hard—no way you're getting this one. Can you say 'extremely random'?"

Motioning his hands he said, "We'll see about that."

Molly announced the third and final song and placed the paper Emma had written on in the middle of the table face down. This time knowing it would be a challenge, Drew closed his eyes and listened to a song by the group Diamond Rio, 'One More Day.'

He was dying listening to the words because he had never heard it without thinking of Emma. He was surprised she picked it because she'd never listened to country music, and although Taylor Swift was country, she was also considered a crossover artist. He asked to listen a second time because honestly, the first was more like a gut punch he had to hide from everyone.

His eyes had been closed, but they opened as the song approached the second chorus. He looked directly into Emma's eyes as if no one else were in the room. Then, without missing a beat, he sang the words as the music paused. "One more day, one more time," and at the end of the word *time*, he played his air piano and said, "There it is, Em. There is your part."

He was dead on, again. Neither of them could deny the deep soul connection they clearly still had. No one could, but it just wasn't meant to be. It was more than Emma could take, and for the second time that night, she had to get out because she thought she might be sick. She was so thankful she was staying just next door.

"Well, you are *something*, Drew Dalton, I must say. And also, it's late, and *I still* have packing to do. Also, I have to get some sleep if I am driving back tomorrow."

She once again said her goodbyes, but this time, Drew walked over and pulled her away from the others.

This time, Darby was in the perfect position to observe them as they interacted.

"Em, before you leave in the morning, I want you to do something with me."

"I really don't think—" she began, but he simply put his fingers over her mouth and continued in a soft whisper almost.

"Meet me at The Point before you leave. I want to discuss a few ideas."

She started to protest, but her heart was too exhausted, and all her defenses were down at this point. He had too much of her to argue tonight, so she reluctantly agreed.

"Okay then, Em. I will see you at eight in the morning, or eight-ish. 'Em time'."

She shook her head because she had run out of words. She was finally able to muster up a "Goodnight, Drew" as she looked intently into his soul-piercing blue eyes. So many questions were still left unanswered and that familiar ache of yesterday returned.

Drew simply pulled her into him and buried her head in his chest as he closed his eyes and kissed the top of her hair whispering, "Goodnight, Em." Without even looking at her again, he walked away.

When he let go, she waved goodnight to the crowd and left. She quickly escaped because that had depleted her last ounce of strength. She made it safely into the shop next door before breaking down, but this time, Jane was fast on her heels.

Chapter Eight

*"True love leaves a memory that no one can steal,
And a heartache that no one can heal."
~Author Unknown*

JANE WALKED INTO the shop to find Emma sitting on the floor in front of the fireplace. The soft glow highlighted the pain shown on her dear friend's face as a stream of tears poured down her cheeks. She was sitting there in the gigantic sweatshirt of the man she clearly still loved.

When Emma closed her eyes and buried her nose into the grey fabric, it was almost as if he were right there with her. Then, she wrapped herself inside the oversized sleeves and began to sob. Immediately, Jane rushed to her, and Emma fell over in her lap, crying uncontrollably.

"It's okay, honey. Just let it out. Cry all you want. Nothing is better than getting the cry out. And from the look and sound of this, you have held a lot of 'cry' in for some time now." Jane let her friend lie with her head in her lap while she said nothing except an occasional "It's okay" while softly patting her back.

Her mom walked in because she heard the commotion from upstairs. Jane was quiet tonight, but her mom was ready to talk. She had been waiting for this.

"I will make some coffee." Ella left but was back with coffee shortly.

EMMA WAS NOT the only one having a life altering moment. Just next door, Darby stood staring at a quote on Mazi's wall as Drew told his friends goodnight. When he returned inside, he told the waitress she could leave and he would lock up behind her before he went to sleep upstairs for the night.

The bells jingled as she closed the door. Drew walked behind Darby and kissed her neck saying, "Now I finally have you all to myself." When he looked up, he realized she was in deep thought, and her eyes were moist with tears, which was followed by a moment of realization.

She read from the wall aloud, "'We are shaped and fashioned by what we love,' Johanne Wolfgang von Goethe.' You wrote that on this wall in 2002, Drew," she said while wiping a single tear as it rolled down her cheek. "What are your dreams, Drew?" Her eyes now were collecting fresh tears.

"Honey, what are you talking about? Where is this all coming from?" He tried to pull her into him, but she refused and pushed him slightly.

"Just answer the question, Drew," she calmly replied as he led her to the couch on the other side of the fountain bar.

Seeing how shaken and completely serious she was, he began to answer stroking her hand with his thumb, "To eventually build my own sound equipment business and possibly have a recording studio here in town, I suppose. You know that though. Darby, what's wrong, baby?" he asked with a gnawing sense of dread in the pit of his stomach.

"Okay, and what are the rest of your dreams?" she asked followed by a long, unnatural silence. After what seemed like forever she pressed again for a response, "Please, Drew. I need you to say it out loud to me. I need to hear you say the words. *You* need to hear you say the words. It's time to be honest."

"You know, we are going to remodel the old mansion and make it a place for the community," he stated without actually making eye contact with her.

"Okay. Answer me this," she asked in a breathless whisper. "What point in your life did you realize your dreams, Drew? Who helped you discover them? When were they awakened inside of you?"

"Where is all this coming from? You know…"

"Just please, Drew. I need you to answer the question."

"Okay. Let's see." She could see his facial expression go from tense to carefree as soon as he found his own 'remember when' place. "You know, I never really thought about it. It just was something I always *knew*. When Emma and I were young, I mean like eight, nine, ten young, we would put plays together for the other neighborhood kids." He was drifting to some unfamiliar place to her as he spoke. "Em would write these crazy plays and cast any kid that was willing to let her boss them." He paused and smiled a little, not realizing all the things his eyes were giving away as he got lost in the past.

He continued, "Emma had our moms make fliers and drive her around for blocks passing out those things door to door. We had converted the huge front porch of the old mansion into a stage. She said it reminded her of the Orpheum with those majestic, tall, white columns set amongst all the decorative wood. I remember her little plays always drew a crowd, and some were actually pretty good." He looked at Darby with a half-smile and laughed.

Darby listened and watched him totally transform to someone she didn't recognize. The man she was afraid he truly was. A man that tried but had never really belonged to her. This man did, and always had, belonged with another. Emma. He belonged with Emma.

"She had my dad haul a generator up there so she would have a microphone — that *I* was to set up, of course. My daddy would do just about anything for his 'Emmy Em'. So, that is when I assume my quest for the perfect sound began," he said with a mysterious vagueness. "Funny, I hadn't thought of that in years."

Devastated, she continued her line of questioning. "And what about The Point? The gardens? Where did that dream come from, Drew?" The tears flowed freely down her cheeks now. She no longer even tried to hold them back.

"Darby, where is this coming from?" he pleaded.

"Just answer the question, please, Drew. I need to know. I have to know."

"Darby…"

"Drew. Drew, please."

His eyes finally locked with hers as one simple word fell on his heart. *Emma*. He could not lie to Darby.

Finally, the words found their way from his heart to his lips, and he spoke. "Emma. It came from Emma. Well, the two of us. Darby, you have to understand. We have always been friends. Our families are so close. We grew up together."

"How is it I never knew any of this? No one prepared me or shared with me the bond the two of you have. Drew, you shared much more than dreams with her—you were in love with her—deep love— your first love." Taking a few calming breaths, she continued. "First loves, when they are deep and real, well, they never really die."

Pulling her close and kissing her lips playfully to lighten the mood, he responded, "Ah, but true love— true love can bury it alive."

She stepped back from him saying, "Unless they happen to be the same person."

"No, Darby. That was ages ago. You are the *only* one. I love you, Darby. You."

She continued after pausing to gather her composure, "I think you believe that— but you don't see what I see, Drew. You have never looked at me the way you look at her. You look at each other way past the eyes. You see each other's souls or something. You have single handedly created a 'garden of Eden' that's a tribute to her. It's your dream with her, not me. It was 'shaped by what you love' just like the quote says that you wrote on that wall years ago. Actions speak volumes, and *you* are the only one who ever calls her Em. Did you notice that, Drew? I did. One day, and I picked right up on that."

"Darby, that was our childhood playground," he said lifting his hand in the air. "Of course it's tender to my, our hearts, but you and I are together now."

"Drew, do you even know *my* favorite song… much less, just know my favorite part of it just because you know *me*? Do you know how I want *my* favorite drink or even *what* it is?" By the look on his face, she knew her answer. Drew handed her a tissue as she continued. "Drew, you love her. You may not be ready to admit it, but you loved her then, and you love her now. I have seen you melt in her presence this weekend just when she comes near you. She's all over you. Can't you see that? You are still lost inside her somewhere, and I think it's time you go find you."

"I am sorry if you feel…"

"Stop, Drew. Just stop," she said staring off into the unknown. He listened intently as her voice became barely audible. "You know, if I am honest, I always knew there was a part of you missing. I didn't know until this weekend what it even was. I know now though, Drew," she continued through a steady stream of tears." It's your heart. Your heart's missing. She's your other half. Face it."

Now tears formed in his eyes as the truth somehow forced them out with each word Darby spoke. "Drew, in love we deny the truth sometimes, many times actually. We deny it because in reality it's often too painful for us to see. Saying it or even acknowledging it may be more than we think we can take, but I believe that *not* acknowledging it is a far worse fate. You owe it to you, you owe it to me, and you owe it to Emma to follow your heart. I think you will find that it will lead you straight to her."

After a long, long silence, Drew spoke. "Darby, I don't know what to say."

Feeling surprisingly stronger and renewed, she said, "Say I am right."

He could only shake his head yes as he wiped a few loose tears off his face.

Then she took her engagement ring off her finger, placed it in his hand, and kissed it. "I am going to get my things and head out tonight. I have a lot to sort out in my mind." She stood and took a deep breath. "Drew, I love you. I really do," she said, trying not to be emotional. "But I deserve to be loved for the quirky little things, too. I want to be loved in details the way you obviously love her. I want to be someone's Emma."

"You deserve someone who can love you completely—with all they have, not just fragments of themselves. Darby, I do love you—just not the way I should. I am so sorry. I never meant to hurt you,"

"I know, I know. It's okay. I will be okay. You are right. I deserve someone's entire heart—someone that actually has one to give. You gave yours away a long time ago. Now, go find it."

As she gathered her things and kissed his cheek goodbye, he held her for a long time, as they stood in one another's arms and cried. It was easier to avoid the truth and far less painful. Finally, they released from the embrace and said their good-byes.

As Darby headed for the door, she turned and said one more thing to him, "Tell her how you feel, Drew. Don't let your pride, Julie, or anything else stop you. She loves you, too. It shows all over her face. Goodbye, Drew."

With those words, Darby Spencer was gone. She left Drew alone and she'd given him much to think about. What was he supposed to do now?

Chapter Nine

*"Truth is like the sun—you can shut it out for a time,
But it ain't goin' away."*
~Elvis Presley

Jane and Mama El made Emma go upstairs, and they all sat on Emma's bed with cups of coffee. It had been years since they had sat there and talked on this bed, but this time, it was not for sentimental reasons. This was an emergency intervention long past due, and no one was leaving until Emma gave them honest answers.

Emma placed her cup on the nightstand by her bed and curled up between her mom and Jane. She was still snuggled in Drew's oversized sweatshirt. With every breath, she inhaled his scent, and if she closed her eyes, she could almost make herself believe he was lying beside her.

"Okay, Emma, you have to talk," her mom finally said, breaking the silence.

With soft sobs, she said, "I really don't feel there is anything to say. It is what it is."

"What *is it* though, Emma?" Jane inquired. "What happened between you two *before* you left for school? What made you two so estranged—so distant?"

"Emma, we love you. Talk to us, sweetie," her mom said as she gently brushed the hair away from her daughter's face. Emma remained silent. "Okay, then,"

THE *Point*

her mom continued, "I have something to say." Emma didn't move but listened intently.

"Sweetheart, I have watched you grow up. You have a tendency to hide from the things that hurt you, and you always have. Unfortunately, the very one that could always rescue you from your pain is the one you need to be rescued from this time. Oh honey, there comes a time in everyone's life when you just have to take a good hard look at everything. Do you realize I was *your a*ge when your father died in that plane crash?"

Ella paused a moment remembering then continued. "I was crazy scared out of my mind. I had no idea where to go or what to do. I was so lost, but I had the greatest gift of all, and that, my love, was you. I had known true love with your father, I had you, and I had the greatest friends anyone could ever wish for. My life changed in a breath, but I never regretted anything. Do you know why? Because a long time ago, I had to make some hard choices concerning a broken heart too, and I chose to live.

"Life happens only once, so live. Take chances. Most importantly, love. Just love. Yes, it hurts to be honest and to be rejected, but life happens to us all. To not live, though, or to keep yourself from feeling, well, you might as well be dead because really, you *are* if you choose that life." Emma didn't move.

Then her mom shared one more bit of wisdom. "I also realize, on this side of life, the pain, the hard times—it all helped shape me into who I am today. Even though we fall, bend, and yes— sometimes even break— it all works together along with all the wonderful things in our lives to make us who we are and who we are meant to be, sweetheart."

With another deep intake of Drew's scent on his shirt, Emma sat up and gathered her thoughts and emotions before she spoke. "I love Drew. I always have, and I probably always will. But..." she said choking up a little, "he made his choice too, Mom—a long time ago. I remember. I remember every detail."

Emma eased back into the most tender place in her heart—the place where Drew was—the place where she and Drew still were. Her entire countenance changed as she entered into their world.

She continued, "I remember our night before I left for that summer as if it was yesterday. I had mixed feelings about going because I didn't want to be so far away from home and all of you, but especially from him. Summer seemed like forever in my mind. You know, cell phones were new—nothing like they are today. I thought I'd die. My heart hurt so badly, but I wanted to travel. I wanted to see were my dad spent his last days. That Drew," she laughed to herself, "he knew me too well. That day was perfect. That night was *perfect*." She remembered as tears freely fell from her eyes.

"Drew, I know where we are. Come on, why do I have to be blindfolded?"

"I knew we were at The Point. I knew the place by heart. The feel—the smell," she said in a daze.

"Emma, trust me. It's worth it. Just hold onto my hands. Just a little more. Watch your step."

"When he lifted the blindfold, I could not believe how *beautiful* everything was. He had draped all the old, broken furniture in the great room of the mansion in white, linen sheets. There were white lighted candles all around the room, and in the center was, sorry Mom, a bottle of wine chilling that he had stolen from Mrs. Liza and Daddy D's cellar. He had a single candle beside it, and we had oversized pillows for chairs. He had two glasses, and right amongst it all was a small vase of yellow daffodils—my favorite flowers. I was speechless, overwhelmed."

Emma closed her eyes and transported back to that night.

"Drew, when? How?"

"Earlier today—and because I am fabulous like that. So, do you like it?"

"No, I love it." She leaned over and kissed his hand. *"This is unbelievable—like a fairy tale."*

"Good, because you are my princess, and you belong in a fairy tale where all your dreams come true." He gently gave her a quick kiss on the lips and said, *"I love you, Em."* Then, he grabbed her blue jeans at her waist, pulled her into his large, muscular arms, and kissed her until her knees were weak.

"So?" she asked. *"Do you want me to change my plans and never leave, or what?"* They sat on the blanket leaning on the large pillow beside her.

Nervously pouring the wine he said, *"This is to just celebrate you, us—your chance to travel. Em, you have always wanted to go to Greece. How freaking cool is that? Getting the chance to go on the commercial shoot with that advertising agency is a chance in a lifetime. Who knows what doors it will open?"*

"But I don't want a door to open that you aren't on the other side of, Drew. I can't." Tears streamed down her face, and Drew kissed each one.

"Emma," he said breathlessly. "Emma, I will always be with you." He put his hand on her chest feeling her heartbeat. "I am right inside your heart. I am that beat right there. Feel it? That is the reminder that I love you, and every time you feel your heartbeat, remember that is how long I will love you."

Then, he placed her hand on his chest over his heart. "Feel that? That's you, Emma. You are my heart, my soul. You are the love of my life, and as long as I have a beating heart and breath in me, that's how long I will love you. We are timeless." Then, he traced her face as if he were memorizing every single detail. Then he placed her glass beside them on the floor, reached his hand out to help her up, and said, "May I have this dance?"

Laughing, she said, "There is no music."

His reply was hushed. "Yes there is, Em." He gently cradled her in his arms placing her ear against his chest, speaking with an unassuming grace. "Don't you hear it?"

They danced in the glow of the candles, right in the middle of their own special place—both wishing they could melt into one another and make time stop.

Unfortunately, life had to go on whether they wanted it to or not. Being from a single parent family, this opportunity could land her a full scholarship, and she had to take this trip. Besides, Greece had been the last place her dad had been, and part of her was drawn there. Plus, her writing was in dire need of adventures outside the borders of Leyton. Although the inspiration she found in Drew was effortless and flowing, she knew it was time to broaden her writing endeavors beyond her love for him.

He closed his eyes and clinched his jaw trying to fight his tears. Then they stopped dancing as he kissed her forehead, then her cheek, and down her neck. They became lost in each other for the next hour or so. They lay on the floor wrapped in the blanket, holding on to this moment as long as they possibly could.

They talked about her trip and all the things she would see. She knew it killed him to let her go, but as he held her in his arms, she knew he was trying to memorize every single part of her. Sometimes love requires letting go.

Once again, he drew her closer, and as they became one, each poured all they had into the other. They fell asleep in one another's arms on the floor that night. The candles burned down, and the light ceased to be, but the fire inside them, they knew would never die. The love they shared, that soul connection — they knew would last forever.

As the orange pierced through the window the next morning, they knew they would be in trouble for spending the night together, but neither cared. This would get them through the summer. It was worth getting into trouble as far as they were concerned. That was the most beautiful memory they had ever made, and it would be safe in one another's hearts, keeping them bound for longer than either could have imagined.

As they were about to leave, she began to cry, and as he wiped her tears away, he said, "Emma, I love you with all I am. Never forget that. I will always, always love you. I don't know how not to love you. Even though you will be far away, remember, your heartbeat, that's me in there." He placed his hand once more on her heart. "Now, keep me inside your heart and go see the world, Emma Ashby. Then you come back and tell me all about it. Deal? We can do this, Em."

Emma physically shook as she remembered the enormity of the love they shared. She knew they had been entirely too young and should not have crossed that line but also she knew it had been real. It was evident that she still felt the same way. The sadness returned to her eyes as she remembered her present reality.

Ella and Jane hurt for her. While sniffing into a tissue, Jane spoke up saying, "So, what happened after that? How did you guys go from that to now?"

In a distant fog, Emma responded to her friend. "I ask myself the same thing, Jane, all the time. It's easy not to think about it when I'm away from here, but there's no way to escape when I'm here—especially now that he lives next door," she said darting her eyes to both of them, " but I realized this weekend that running from my past is not the same as dealing with it. I have hidden long enough."

"True. You do have a broken-in pair of running shoes, no doubt," her mom added. "But what changed, sweetie? You need to go back if you are ever going to be able to move forward. You have spent so much time hiding, you have forgotten what is normal. It *is* possible to spend so much time stuck in yesterday that you forget about today, and when a person does that, they never get to see tomorrow. Trust me… life it too short."

Emma's mind drifted and she said, "You know, when your heart is shattered into so many different pieces, it's really hard to know which piece to follow.

THE *Point*

You don't really—you just sort of get lost somewhere amongst them. That's where I have been for so long now—lost."

Jane and Ella sat silently, waiting for her to continue. She soon continued her tender monologue.

"Well, you know how homesick I was that summer, remember?" she said glancing at her mom. "The few times I actually got to talk to Drew, he encouraged me to stay, and he promised he'd be there waiting when I got home, but the distance was really hard on us — harder than we both imagined." She sat up and began to talk as if no one else was in the room. "Although Greece, the commercial shoot, and the internship were all a dream come true, one thing became evident to me that summer: without Drew, my dreams didn't matter. He was at the center of them all. There I was in the most amazing place, and all I could write about was Drew. I knew then. *He* was my inspiration."

When she remembered Jane and her mom, she snapped back into the moment and continued. "Still, the offer Mr. Barlow had presented me with was amazing. A full four-year scholarship, a part-time job with a company writing, and with a guarantee to have a full-time position upon graduating, how could I have honestly walked away? I was so confused. Remember?" she looked at both of them as they sat on edge wondering what she was finally about to reveal.

They both hung on her every word and nodded yes.

"Anyway, when I finally got home at the beginning of August, I only had a short time to make my decision. Drew had lost his phone so he left word for me, with you, Mom, to call his home phone." She smiled as if she was looking at the memory in a photo album. "Just hearing his voice and knowing I was about to look into those beautiful blue eyes again, well my heart knew the answer I was looking for; it was there all the time. The answer was right inside me all along, with each beat of my heart—with Drew. I could not wait to see him, to hold him."

"Drew? Hey. It's me. I missed you so much."

"Ahhh, hey, baby. I cannot tell you how great it is to hear your voice," he said relieved and adoringly. "I need to see you. There is so much I have to tell you. Where are you now?"

"Home. Just got here."

Interrupting her, he said, "I can be there in... no, meet me at our place in thirty minutes, and Em, I sure am glad you are back. I am so ready to see you."

"You too, Drew. I love you so much, and I have so much to tell you—and have I got pictures to show you! I'll be there."

"I love you, too."

By the look on her face, the ladies knew the story was about to take a turn in a different direction.

Emma paused to regain her composure. When she was able, she continued. "So, I touched up my hair and makeup, grabbed a few pictures, and left for The Point, our place. It was about six o'clock, so I headed out so I wouldn't be late. I could hardly wait to see him. I would never be away like that again. I knew with perfect clarity that no matter what my future held, it would always include being with Drew. All summer, I had one person after the other tell me we were too young to have such a serious relationship and that I had no clue what true love even was, but I just felt sorry for them. Obviously, they had never known love like Drew and I had or they would recognize it with one glance in my eyes. I felt him all inside me, and how they couldn't see him in me was a mystery."

She stopped to catch a breath and began again. "So, I got there a little early. I brought the gifts I had gotten him and a few letters I had written him with me. I never intended to send the letters, but I wrote him as a way of sorting through the decisions I had to make since I could not just pick up the phone and talk it out. I brought a few photos to show him that I had already printed. I just sat on the porch, *our porch,* remembering how that was our stage when we were little, our place to dream in our early teens, and the place where we first fell in love.

"I had been there a little while and was beginning to get worried because it was almost seven o'clock. I was afraid he had been in an accident. Then my mind wandered. Maybe he hadn't missed me like I missed him. What if he had changed? Did his feelings for me change, too? He had said he loved me on the phone, but what if that was just out of habit. Maybe he wanted to soften the blow. Finally, I heard a car drive up, and I was so relieved. I jumped to my feet, and my heart fell to see that it was only Julie, which made me nervous. I knew something was wrong because Julie practically never came home, and when she did, she certainly didn't come to see me. I panicked, and by the time she made her way to me, I was just sick."

"Hey, Julie. Where's Drew?" She stopped when Julie abruptly interrupted her.

"Emma, I need to talk to you. Come sit down with me."

Panic set in, and Emma asked anxiously, "Is Drew okay? Did something happen? What..."

"No, no he's fine. He is okay. It's just..." She paused as Emma's insides felt as if they were falling out. "Emma, it's just, well, he's not coming."

In shock she asked, "W-w-what? But I just talked to him, He said—"

Again, Julie interrupted her. "Just hear me out. We are contemplating opening a second store here in Leyton, so he and I have reconnected over the summer. It's been a long time since we have had a close relationship. Actually, he was so young when I left, we practically were strangers."

Laughing a bit sarcastically she said, "Besides, in all of his spare time, he was with you. We have had many heart-to-hearts this summer, Emma. He is so precious. He didn't want to hurt you. He would have never been able to tell you all this. Honestly, he wouldn't have mentioned it because he would rather stay with you than see you hurt. The truth is, well, he missed you terribly at the beginning of the summer, but as the time passed, his feelings for you changed. He told me you were more of a friend, a good friend—no, a great friend, but he realized that the love he felt for you was more like the kind he felt for me. Well, you know what I mean.

THE Point

He said he couldn't keep you from your chance at a full scholarship knowing that he didn't really love you — in that way, you know — in love with you. So I told him I would come and talk to you — woman to woman."

Emma sat there in shock for a long time as she tried to process Julie's words. Then she said, "I don't believe you, Julie. He would never avoid telling me something like this in person. It's Drew — my Drew. We have always told each other everything. He loves me, Julie. What we share is — "

Julie abruptly interrupted her saying, "Then if he loves as much as you say he does, where if he now? If I had not spoken to him then just how would I know to find you here of all places?" She was sounding more and more convincing as she continued, "What you had is over. I am sorry that this hurts you, Emma." She placed her hand on top of Emma's. "The best thing for you to do is take that scholarship at the University of Alabama. Leave this town, the past, and Drew behind you. You are such a beautiful young woman. You have a very promising future. Go live your life, Emma, far away from Leyton."

Emma sat for a moment and then said, "No. Drew has to tell me this himself. He would never do this without talking this out with me. I am going to the house. Thanks, but — "

As she stood up, Julie continued talking. "Emma, no. You don't know how hard this summer was on him. He doesn't want to hurt you, so if you go to him, he will come back to you. Is that what you want? Him at any cost? Even if he is miserable? Are you really that selfish? If you really love him the way you claim to, you will walk away and never look back. Do that for him. Do that for yourself. You deserve better — someone that really loves you."

Devastated and broken, she sat in the midst of her shattered dreams, sobbing uncontrollably. That is just what *she had been thinking as she waited. He was not in love with her after all. She had been such a fool to really believe they were really soul mates. All those people were right after all. They were too young.*

Finally, when she was able to speak again, she asked a favor of Julie. "Julie, here are a few things I have for him. Could you please see that he gets them? And please, don't tell him how upset I am, but do tell him I will always love him."

"Okay, sweetie. I will," Julie said as she stroked Emma's hair. "It will be okay. Shhh." Julie hugged her before she stood up. "Goodbye, Emma. I am so sorry about all this. I promise, someday, it will all be okay." Then with a slight wave, she turned and walked away.

Emma got into her jeep and had a complete breakdown throwing her Queen CD into the air while driving off the land as fast as she could. The road was barely visible through her blinding tears, and she soon pulled over on the side of the road because she was sick at her stomach. She was sobbing uncontrollably, grabbing her waist, feeling as if she had just been told that Drew died. She just wanted her Drew. She just wanted to hold him one more time. If she could, she would never let him go again.

Now, THE THREE women sat on the bed, in a pool of tears—speechless.

Chapter Ten

"The heart has its reasons which reasons does Not know."
~Blaise Pascal

EMMA ATTEMPTED TO get ready for her early morning meeting with Drew and Darby. Although, with only two hours of sleep combined with a healthy cry, the task was not working in her favor. She did know, however, that last night was past due. She thought of a quote her mama used to share with her when she was little. "Sometimes people have to cry out all their tears to make room for a heart full of smiles." Well, she did not know for sure about the smiles, but she was certain she had made progress by getting the cry out.

Slipping on khaki shorts, a T-shirt, and her old faithful Yankees cap, she stopped by Mazi's to grab a coffee. She was once again thankful for sunglasses. It looked as if she were seriously hung over, and although she felt like it too, physically, deep inside, she felt surprisingly good. Talking out the past was therapeutic—painful, yes, but so worth it. Today was going to be better—certainly better than last night. So she hopped in her Jeep and drove to The Point.

Just as she pulled off the road to the drive leading up to the house, she spied the Mustang. She smiled remembering all the times they took the top off and drove randomly anywhere just because she loved the wind rushing all around her. It was good to be home, but it was also time for her to leave. She hoped after meeting Drew and Darby this morning, she could go back, say goodbye to her mom and Jane, and head out of town — finally.

She felt better today, but still being in that house was just too much. Especially being in that room with Drew *and* Darby. She could not help remembering the last time she and Drew were in that room together. "Oh my," she said quietly to herself forcing herself not to have a panic attack. "I must be out of my mind, but here goes."

She walked up the familiar, rounded stone steps to the front porch. That massive porch transformed to a stage on many occasions for talent shows and plays that were freely performed for anyone who would attend. Four towering columns that connected past the second floor to the roof held up the porch's structure. Emma smiled looking up at the French doors that lead out onto the balcony of the second floor. Thoughts about how she used to dream of standing on that overlook imagining she was a princess looking down upon her kingdom filled her mind. She was glad that the second floor would be accessible again since the renovations would restore the spiral staircase to its former glory.

Standing just outside the white double doors with the glass pane windows above and down each side, she took a few deep breaths and then knocked on the door. While waiting on someone to come to the door, she thought about all the memories she and Drew made on that front porch. She was so absorbed in thought that when Drew answered the door, not only did she jump, but she also blushed as if he could see straight through to her mind. Breathlessly she simply said with a slight wave of her hand, "Here I am."

"Hey, Em. Come on in," he said with a rather blank tone.

In all the times she had played this possible scenario over in her mind, nothing prepared her heart for the emotion she experienced walking through the doors into that room again. It had been cleaned out and was well into the basic renovations, but for just a brief moment, she merely saw the room draped in white linen sheets with candles all around, and for one heartbreaking moment, she felt the carefully patched-up pieces of her heart come apart. She forced herself to be there in the present and not in the past. With every ounce of strength she could muster, she walked into the room with Drew.

Looking around the room he said, "This is it. It still has a lot of work to go, but it is becoming a reality. What do you think so far?"

Although the construction crew had some equipment and tools lying around, it was as beautiful as she imagined — and as alive as she always knew it could be. "Drew, I think it's just going to be amazing — it already is," she said trying to keep it all about the house without anything personal attached to it. Then, looking around, she asked, "Where is Darby this morning? Hope we didn't overload her with too much information last night," she said with a light half-laugh.

"Darby won't be making it this morning — or any other morning. She uh… she called the wedding off last night."

"What?"

"She gave the ring back. It's over. So, I guess it's just you and me."

"Drew, I…" she didn't know how to process this new information or what to think—or say for that matter. This was completely unexpected and the last thing she expected first thing this morning. She had certainly not had enough coffee and was desperately wishing for more.

"Look, I haven't even had one hour of sleep, Emma. I have no answers—only questions myself. I am tired. I am more tired than you could possibly know," he said looking away "This entire weekend… Anyway, I just can't talk about this now."

"Drew, do you really think I am the right one for this? It really doesn't seem…"

He interrupted her saying, "Emma, I am twenty-seven years old, single, as of last night, and I am *still* trying to find out parts of myself that have been missing for so long. I don't even know where to look anymore—or what to look for exactly, but there is *one* thing I know more than I know my name, and that is this fact. This house is somehow directly connected to my heart. All I have are memories, it seems."

He paused, attempted a laugh, and then continued. "My cherished and most special memories were made in and around this house. Most of my entire, young life was lived right here. Who I am—the *me* I am trying to find, was formed on this very foundation—on this very land—on this very point."

He paced across the room and ran his fingers through his hair, letting out a sigh of frustration as he continued. He looked up at Emma. "*That* is what I am trying to figure out—the point—*my* point. Like

THE *Point*

I said, I don't have anything now but questions, but somehow, this place," he said looking about the room and gesturing with his hands, "holds the answers. Em, I don't want to talk about the past. I am too tired—my soul is even tired. Besides, the past has passed, but we grew up together. We were best friends, and no one knows me the way you do," he said as his voice choked into a whisper and tears caught inside his throat.

"Or did," he added. "Yesterday, I was going to ask you to advise and help bring the house back to life — for the community. For whatever my reasons were, or are, I'm not sure, but that was *literally* yesterday. Today, it's personal," he said with a half-laugh. "I guess it was always personal. Darby somehow figured it out in one weekend—what I have tried to piece together for so long, but now, I need my friend, Emma, to help her old friend, Drew, find the answers."

A silence fell around them. He sat down in the floor in a foggy haze. "I'm lost, Em. Help me find my way back. Help me with the house, please?" he looked up at her helplessly with his red, sleep-deprived eyes as they filled with tears.

She walked over and sat beside him. "What exactly are you asking from me, Drew?"

"Help me bring this house back to life. Help me remember the way we dreamed it could be when we were kids, and maybe it'll bring me back to life, too." He was quiet for a moment and then spoke again saying, "I'll tell you what. Think it over for a couple days — or a week or however long it takes for you to say yes. Just let me know." He sounded so defeated. So lost.

Before she could answer, he perked up a little and

asked, "Have you got a little more time?"

Looking at the time she said, "Maybe a little, but I really need to get on the road soon."

"It won't take too long, but I really want to show you something before you leave or make up your mind."

She smiled and nodded her head yes and followed Drew out the back way. They walked outside, and he smiled as he helped her in his Polaris Ranger.

The grounds were nicely groomed and well kept. As they drove by the park walking track, again she could see day lilies and her favorite little yellow flowers sprinkled throughout the place in the distance. Her view was from the opposite direction this time, and she could see just how many daffodils there actually were.

Then they continued past that area and entered another. The apple blossoms were in full bloom, and then beyond that, she could see the pecan trees that were planted by Drew's great grandfather in the early 1900s. His mother planted the apple trees when Drew was a baby, and now they seemed to produce the most delicious apples in the area. People even came from surrounding areas to load up on Mrs. Liza's apples. Families came; schools made field trips out of visiting the orchard, and local restaurants used only the homegrown apples for their creations. One of their best customers was the owner of the Rolling Pin Bakery. That lady could think of more uses for an apple than anyone Drew had ever known — besides his mom. Many other local and nearby businesses bought in bulk, but what Emma loved most was the scent. It is what she always thought happy smelled like. She related it to her childhood when her daddy would bring her to pick apples — that was one of the most vivid memories she had of him.

She smiled, and they continued as Drew pointed out little things along the way until they finally stopped and looked right ahead. "Look, Em."

Squealing like a little girl, she jumped out of the Ranger and ran into the grassy field of daffodils that led right to the edge of 'their' lake — 'their' pier that now had a cabin built just beyond it. "Drew. I *love* this. You always said you would build a cabin out here. This is amazing."

"I *knew* you would love it. This is a private area back here and restricted to the public. *This* is all mine."

"Why the heck are you living above Mazi's café and not here then?"

"Honestly, Darby wasn't a fan. She is great, sweet, and kind, but the outdoors, well, let's just say it's not her thing. She didn't see what I see here. Deep down, I don't even know if I wanted her to. This is sacred ground to me," he said with a look that made Emma wonder what was going on in that head of his. He then walked across the room and said, "Come check it out," as if he was a child again wanting to show his friend everything all at once.

Inside, it was just a simple rustic cabin, but not lacking personality. One large room with rustic furniture, a TV, a large picnic-type table, and a kitchen nook in the far corner. Off from the room, a small hall led to the bathroom, and to the left of the bathroom was the only bedroom. The old, iron bed and a few antique pieces continued to reflect the personality of the rest of the cabin.

"This is great, Drew. It's incredible actually." As

they walked back into the main room, Emma spied his guitar and laughed. "Did you ever learn to play *any* song on that?" she asked pointing to the guitar.

"Actually, I did learn to finally play one—just one, but maybe someday I will learn a few more."

He opened the door, and they walked back outside and sat down on the pier. Before Emma knew it, she had kicked her shoes off and had her feet dangling off into the pond. Then, Drew joined her. Sitting with their feet in the water seemed to relax them both. For a little while, they forgot about the rest of the world as they always did on that land and that special lake.

"Remember when we were fishing out here with Daddy D that time and you fell in?" Emma asked.

"You *pushed* me in."

"I bumped *into* you by *accident*." She laughed her mischievous laugh he loved so much.

"Yeah, I remember 'bumping' into you next. We were soaked and so we decided to just jump back in."

"Daddy D never took us fishing again either—said we were too loud."

"Em, you talked the *entire* time. You talked so *loud* and *often*, the fish didn't bite for over a month Dad said." He jabbed her side with his elbow and splashed water on her with his foot.

"Oh no you didn't," she said while splashing him back with excitement.

"What are you going to do about it?" he asked with a much larger splash and a real laugh.

"This." Then the splash fight became an all-out water war.

She, being half his size, laughed uncontrollably when he came over and lifted her into his arms, throwing her over his shoulder like a sack of potatoes. As she kicked her feet and playfully screamed and laughed, he moved to cradle her in his arms and held her like a baby—or more like a wild toddler. Then he smiled and threw her off the edge of the pier and jumped in behind her.

"No!" she exclaimed. "I cannot believe you did this!" Then she lunged into him with flailing arms, reverting back into adolescent mode.

They had a classic Drew/Emma water wrestling match right there in the lake. Dunking, splashing, and laughing—the kind of laughter that only comes from a place deep inside—the kind that melts the world away, for a little while, at least. Finally, they called a truce and climbed back onto the pier. He stepped inside to get towels and threw one at her.

"Wow," she said still smiling. "That was fun. I haven't played like that in years."

"You know, me either." Then they looked at each other, and he asked, "Are you thinking what I'm thinking?"

"Let's do it. I'll race you," she yelled.

Then, like two children, they raced to the field that led to Leyton Falls, just beyond the family property line. Actually, it streamed from a larger waterfall that flowed down from the Smokies. Although it was a much smaller scaled waterfall than the powerful one it originated from, the water still cascaded over a mountain of rocks and was one of the most beautiful places in Leyton. After a big rain, the water was incredible as it rushed from the rocks into a lagoon. It was one of the best-kept secrets, too. Since it was adjacent to their land, few people really knew it was there.

Just as they hit the daffodils running, Drew insisted on stopping for a minute. He stooped down to pick a yellow flower for Emma and placed it behind her ear, allowing her hair to brush against it. She could not only see, but could actually feel his eyes linger at her a bit too long. Every time he looked into her eyes, it seemed he had to pry himself away. What was he thinking? Damn him. She pretended not to notice the want in his eyes and curtsied as she accepted the flower. She simply smiled, and they were off again—until they heard someone calling Drew's name. As they turned around, they saw Julie pulling toward them in the golf cart.

"Why if it's not the two 'most wanted' in their secret hideaway together, *again*," she said in a lofty tone while daggers shot from her eyes. "You two always did like to sneak off down here in this filthy, muddy bottom. Some things never change, do they?" She shot a direct look at Emma.

Reality came crashing back as she stood face to face with Julie. All of it. How humiliating to get swept up in the moment like this. She was certain her neck was getting blotches on it again.

"Drew, I think I'll take a rain check on the falls if you don't mind," Emma said. How ridiculous they were—acting like children again, at their age—acting as if they had no past, no breakup. She continued, "I think I will just walk on back."

"No Emma. You take the Ranger, and I'll get Julie to run me back in the cart."

"Okay, thanks," she reluctantly replied. "And by the way, I love the place. You did good, Drew Dalton."

She gave him a wry smile.

"I'm glad you like it, Miss Emma," Drew said.

"Well, goodbye," she said trying to keep any emotion from showing. "And I had fun. Thank you. I needed this today." Then she turned toward Julie and said, "Julie, it was," she paused and then continued, "well it was *something* seeing you again." That was the only thing she could think to say that would not be a complete lie.

Drew walked toward her and suddenly grabbed her hand, pulled her back around toward him, and said, "I *will* be in touch soon, and hey, thanks for today. I needed today, too." He gave her a quick wink and smile that poured all over her body like rain.

Looking back at him and then at Julie, Emma simply said, "Okay," and shook her head yes. Then, with a final goodbye wave, she left.

As soon as Emma was out of Julie's earshot, she tore into his poor soul. "Drew Dalton, what are you thinking?" she asked in anger. "That *woman* has not caused you *anything* in your life but heartache. Have you forgotten just how badly she completely shattered your heart and left you devastated that summer she returned from Greece?"

"No, Jules. No, and if I did, you have always been there to remind me. Every time she is even in the vicinity—you *always* seem to remind me."

"And Darby? You broke off the engagement?"

"Get your facts straight, lady. *She* broke that off."

"But you *let* her because of *her*," Julie yelled.

Julie's resentment of Emma had worsened over the years, which no one understood. However, Julie had always adored her little brother like her own child. She was overprotective, but now she was becoming obsessive over his love life.

He could not deny the bond he still had with Emma. The history was there, of course, but that was not all. Whatever he had shared with her was still there. The longing to just get lost in her was stronger than ever. He knew Emma had caught him stealing glances at her. He was not good at hiding anything from her, and this was getting harder by the moment.

She continued her lecture, but her words just drifted around him. He was no longer in that moment — he was in the old mansion. He thought back and remembered each heartbreaking moment of that day as if it happened yesterday…

Drew stepped inside the old place and was startled to see his sister. "Julie? What are you doing here? Where's Emma?" he asked holding a single daffodil in his hand.

"Drew, um, you need to come over and sit down for a minute."

The blood drained from his face, and panic set in. "Emma. Has something happened to her? Is she okay?"

"Just sit down. There has not been an accident or anything. She is okay."

"Well, where did she go? Does she want me to meet her at the shop? I knew I was taking too long—"

Julie jumped right into his sentence and said abruptly, "She's not coming Drew. She left, and I don't think she's coming back."

"What?" He paused for a brief second. "No… I just…"

"Listen to me Drew. Listen. She is not coming back. She asked me to tell you something. Come. Sit down."

"W-w-hat?" he asked mindlessly as he sat down running his fingers through his hair feeling like the wind had been knocked out of him.

"Drew, there is no easy way to say this, but Emma doesn't love you anymore—not romantically I mean. She didn't know how to tell you, so she asked me to tell you for her."

A look of confusion came over him then he said, "Not funny, Julie. Where is Emma?"

"I told you. She left, Drew."

"What are you talking about, Julie? You two aren't even friends. You don't even know her."

"I stopped by, like you said, to tell her you were running late. I told her how I had gotten caught up with the carpenters at the shop and had to ask you to run an errand for me. I had no idea you'd have to wait almost an hour," she lied. "Sorry. Anyway, it was just as well, Drew. She was cold about it all, actually. She handed me this shirt and asked me to give it to you. Then she asked me to tell you she was sorry, but she realized this summer that there were great adventures in this world, and she needed to see as many as possible. She said more, but that was the main part. She rambled something about seeing the world through her father's eyes or something. I am so sorry, Drew," she said patting his back.

"No," he simply replied broken and hushed. "Not Emma — not my Em. She would never leave without saying goodbye to me, or talking to me about this. No, I'm going to *talk to — to see her."*

She couldn't believe how they each said almost the identical thing. It made her sick that they loved each other so much.

Grabbing his hand Julie pleaded in her craftiness, "Don't, Drew. Emma did say that she would have never been able to say these things to your face and she would have kept things the same. That's why she left before you came. So, if you go to her, she'll change her mind and stay with you, but out of pity. If you really, really love her the way you say you do, then let her go. If you two are meant to be, really meant to be, eventually, you will find each other again. If not, it's good you let go now. Let her go, Drew. It's for the best, sweetie."

There was no way he was not going to talk this out face to face and was about to say so until Julie interrupted him mid-sentence.

He said, "But—"

Then Julie interrupted saying, "Drew, she dropped something when she left. Something fell out of her purse. I picked it up thinking it was trash, but I think you should see this. It may explain a few things."

The first thing he saw in the papers she handed him was a picture of Emma and a group of other interns from Barlow and Stallings in front of The National Archeological Museum in Athens. The second photo, however, caught his attention. It was a picture of her and some guy on a beach. Looking on the back it said, 'Emma and Alec, beautiful shore of the Aegean Sea.' It pained him to see her looking so happy with anyone besides him. This made him wonder if Julie was actually telling him the truth, but why would she ever make up anything that would devastate him like this? The next item he saw confirmed it. It was in Emma's handwriting too.

It looked like only part of a letter, and some of it was

clearly missing, but the message was clear. He read aloud.

"'I am too young to know what real love truly is. I need to enjoy my life. I need to travel, date other people, and see all of the world I can while I am young. The only thing I have holding me back is myself. I hope you can comprehend what I am saying to you, Drew.'"

There was no other part of the letter. Simple, yet to the point, and in her own handwriting—it was enough to confirm all that Julie had said.

He left the room and started running. He ran all the way down to the lake. His brokenness went deep, deep inside him. He felt with each breath, it might be his last.

"Drew? Drew?" He snapped back into the moment.

"Julie, I remember. I simply want her input on the mansion—that's all. She had the same vision as I did. It is business—strictly business. That's all."

"Well, I hope you are not that ridiculous to fall for her schemes again. She will love you and leave you again. You deserve the very best, Drew. Someone who will—"

Drew cut her off saying, "Jules, please. Let it go. I *have* moved on. No, we both have moved on. Emma and I have not and will not be rehashing our past. Besides, she may not even take me up on the offer."

"Well…"

"Well nothing. Take me to my car, you crazy sister of mine." He laughed and hugged her. "Thanks for loving me enough to always look out for me, Jules, but you have nothing at all to worry about. Emma made her choice long ago, and it was not me. We are done."

As she dropped him off and he got into his Mustang, he reminded himself that Julie was right. He had fallen into his old 'Emma habit' again, and he had to keep his guard up. He knew that Julie did not know that he was immune to a second broken heart. He knew it was impossible to break a heart that was already broken, and as far as he could tell, his heart was still in many pieces.

Chapter Eleven

"Friends are like bras, close to your heart and there for support."
~Author Unknown

SITTING AT HER Barlow and Stallings desk, she felt safe again—safe from anything that threatened to expose the hidden places of her deepest memories. Now, she could do what she did best—work.

The Krispie Kritters account had to be wrapped up by the first of June, which left her under a month to perfect the campaign and give production the go-ahead to begin shooting commercials. She sighed a deep breath of relief at the mere idea of being swamped with work and with no time to think of anything else—especially Drew. The break was short lived, however, when Alec Gresham popped his head into her door.

"Knock, knock," he said barging inside and making himself at home.

"Hey, Alec. Go away. You know I'm busy, you pest."

"Oh, no. I know you well. Remember? I'm not only your ex, but I happen to be the *only* friend you have in Tuscaloosa." Then he laughed and said, "I am also *one* out of the *only* two friends you even have. I know when you are avoiding me. It always means you are hiding something."

"You're right. It's sad, but true," she said. She

stopped and looked at him and said, "That's kinda pathetic isn't it?" She laughed with him. "But, there is nothing to tell. I went home. They dedicated the building, and I came home. Now, if you will excuse me…"

"Emma, you disappoint me. You do know that I can have Jane on speed dial within the next minute, don't you? So, talk. You don't fool me, baby. Come on, it's me."

She actually put her pencil down, and said, "Okay. You're right. There may be a *few* details I left out." Then she proceeded to give him a play by play of the weekend.

"I *knew* it. See, that wasn't so bad was it?" he asked gently then rhetorically asked, "What kind of fool is that man?"

Emma thought he sounded a little too wistful and was relieved when he quickly reverted back to the friend zone they had worked so hard to establish after their break up. It was true that he had truly loved her but both knew they could never be. She clearly loved someone else, and he finally had the courage to make her admit it. It was painful at first, but they were the rare case that was able to maintain a friendship after a break up. She was so thankful they had agreed to try and be friends. Now, it was hard to really imagine them being anything other *than* friends.

"Yes it *was* that bad, and you are annoying as ever. Besides, I don't like you. Now go away," she said with a large dose of dry humor.

"Okay. Let's talk Julie Scott. What's her deal anyhow?"

"Who knows? I might remember her being nice to

me, *maybe* when I was younger, but who knows? She hates me more every time I see her. She is something else I tell you. She is one scary lady."

"Oh I know. I met her that time she came into your mom's shop when we were visiting, remember? She's a special breed, that's for sure, and yes, she really doesn't like you, that is obvious."

"So, how is your mom, by the way?" he continued with his line of questioning.

"She's good and says hi. Now, go ahead and ask me what you really want to know."

"What?" He tried playing it off while fumbling through some mail on her desk, but Emma knew him as well as he knew her.

"Jane is good too, *and* she's still single." She laughed.

Jane and Alec had gotten to know each other pretty well over the past few years. For some reason, Jane thought she would be breaking some sort of 'friend code' if she actually went out with him, though. Alec felt strange about it too, but Emma couldn't care less. She thought they would be great together actually.

Emma had met Alec the summer she was an intern after senior year. They hit it off, and after college they worked together. When he first asked her out on a date, it just seemed like the right thing to do at the time. One thing led to another, and before they knew it, a few years passed. It was fun, but something was missing. They were truly better friends than lovers, so they decided to just be that. Friends. The best of friends, actually.

Emma loved Alec and Jane very much, and she was not surprised when they met and hit it off instantly. She always thought they were a great match—a math person and a teacher—how natural. She had given up trying to convince them, and now she merely made fun of them about the ridiculous friend-code thing. Truth was, they were both her best friends and she could not think of anyone else she would rather either of them be with than one another, but if she butted into their love life, they tried to butt into hers, so she chose to leave *her* butt out of it and let them figure it out on their own. It was actually quite entertaining.

With a smile he said, "Okay. I am leaving, but I will be back. You have not heard the last of me lady," and gave her a wink. "Have dinner with me tonight."

"I can't."

"Emma, you have to eat. Say yes or I am calling your mom. It's your choice."

"Okay, but leave now. Shoo."

He smiled and closed the door.

THE MONTH WORE on, and everything was going smoothly with the ad campaign. She was so sick of the words of the advertisement tag line, but she was thankful for the distraction. Besides, she would get a trip to the World Series out of it, hopefully to see her Yankees play. June was just around the corner, and she knew she had been hiding behind her work to keep from facing some real issues.

Emma knew it was time to make a decision about the offer to help Drew with the house. She had not mentioned it to her boss, but Alec had, of course. It was a given that she could take the time off considering she

THE *Point*

had never had a real vacation in years. The dedication was the most she had been off of work in the entire time she had been with the company.

The passion she once had for writing had seemed to vanish along with everything else she had left behind. The only thing she ever wrote anymore were advertisements and promotional pieces. Emma certainly never made the time to write because that would require delving into her inner self, and that was strictly off limits. Besides, she was not the same person, so she couldn't possibly be of any assistance to Drew with his endeavor. In her mind, it was already a done deal and the answer that she'd give him was a big, fat no. It was a Friday afternoon so she'd just call him on Monday to break the news.

She wrapped up the last minute details at work and was relieved to be finished with the project. She gathered all her work and placed it on Mr. Barlow's desk. After clearing off her own desk, she gathered her things, reached for the light switch, and proceeded to scream loud enough to wake the dead.

"Oh my gosh. You scared me half to death," she said excitedly to Jane and Alec as she sat down to catch her breath. "What the crap are you two doing here anyway—especially you Jane?" Realizing they were up to something, she smugly asked, "What is going on in those twisted little heads of yours?"

"Em, we are here to intervene on your behalf," Jane said.

"*Intervene* for what?" she asked.

Then Alec chimed in, "About working on the house with Drew. We think you should do it."

"Well, Jane, I'm sorry you drove all this way but—"

"Emma, I have known you all my life—and Drew. You two, well, there is so much history between you both. Don't you think you owe it to him, and yourself, to at least find closure on the past you share?"

"Mmm, let's see… nope. Not really," Emma answered firmly.

"Emma, Jane and I love you very much and care about you. Life is passing you by, and you really don't seem to care, but we all know that deep down, you really do. Since you have been back, you've lost yourself in your work —even more than usual. Honestly, I didn't think that was even possible," he said as a side note. "You are amazing at your job, and when it comes to work, there is no one better, but you pretty much suck at life."

Emma looked at him like she was about to contradict what he said then Jane hit back with her speech.

"Emma, I saw you the weekend you came home. When you are with Drew, magic happens—for you both. You aren't you — the you I know and love — without him. It's like he makes you possible. There is a large piece of you missing, and we think Drew holds the key to getting it back. Look, we aren't saying you have to get back together with the guy or profess your undying love to him. Just work with him on the house and see what happens. Then, at the end of the renovation, if nothing has changed, we will never bother you again. Well, about Drew, that is," she added.

The words lingered in the air as Emma tried to process what Jane had just said.

Alec spoke again saying, "Emma, life is full of risks. Don't be afraid to take one now and then, but be very afraid of not ever taking one at all. What do you say?"

After another lingering silence, finally Emma smiled and agreed with them. "Okay, okay. I'll do it. Just remember, you stick your nose in my business, and I stick mine right back in yours. Remember that?"

"Deal," they said simultaneously.

That was just the welcome mat she needed.

"Okay then, you two need to deal with your own sordid love affair while you're so busy dealing with mine. I think it's about time you guys seriously take a long hard look at what the two of you want out of life as well," she said with a snarky little smile as they all walked out of her office.

They stopped to grab a bite to eat when Jane asked, "Emma, have you talked to your mama?" Before she could answer Jane said, "Of course not. You have been avoiding, I mean, 'working' a lot." She winked at Alec and laughed when Emma rolled her eyes. She continued, "Well, you will never in a million years guess who Calvin Scott has been talking to. Darby."

Emma's eyes widened. "No way. Drew's Darby?" she asked extremely surprised. "I bet Julie loves this," she said while laughing.

"I don't know any details, but Mazi even saw them in the café having lunch one day last week."

"Wonder how Drew is handling that?" she asked in wonder.

"Since you left, all Drew does is work at the house. Besides, he did not love her. He loved, and *still* does love you. I just know it in my gut, and something doesn't add up in all of this."

"Come on guys, it has been seven years. Let it go." Emma said.

"Well, I think Julie had a hand in you two parting.

Something is screwy, and someone needs to find out for sure what happened that day," Jane responded.

"I agree with Jane, Em," Alec added.

"Of *course* you do, Alec. You two have issues. You need to stop avoiding your lives by dictating what I should do in mine."

"No Emma, I am serious. Yes, I agree it's time for the two of us to discuss our relationship options, but I am serious about Julie." He glanced at Jane but continued. "Emma, Julie is certifiable. Something seems extremely off with her as far as you're concerned. You deserve to know the truth. You and Drew both do."

"Thank you for caring, guys, and you're right," she said solemnly. "Maybe I do need this for closure. The renovation of this home may be the only way to get that." She thought about what Drew had said before she left. "In renovating the house, Drew said he needed to find himself. He said he felt lost. I feel it too—lost, like I am searching for something and I don't even know what it is. Does that sound totally weird?"

She knew they were right. The choice was clearly before her. It was time to go back and face whatever it was she had been keeping at bay. It was time to surrender and with a look of defeat, she held up her glass to her best friends and said, "To finding what's lost."

They all drank after the toast. Then she threw in, "and that goes for *you two* as well. Now, if you will excuse me, I have a phone call to make." She smiled and left the restaurant hoping her friends would soon discover what she already knew. They loved each other.

THE Point

EMMA WAS NERVOUS as she got into the Jeep. She left her friends at the restaurant to deal with their own drama, but for now, it was time she dealt with her own. It was time—Alec was right about that.

She picked up her cell to phone Drew, but all she could think about was the day she called him when she arrived back from her trip to Greece. How could she possibly call him again? Look how that turned out. No, she was right the first time. She'd just leave it alone. After all, some things were much better left in the past, and this was surely one of them.

What good would it do to hear him explain that he had outgrown her — outgrown them and their 'forever.' She had barely survived those words the first time, and although she had grown in many ways, her heart had not. She knew it wasn't strong enough to deal with all that again, especially face to face.

She had this ongoing conversation with herself all the way back to her apartment. She had definitely decided to decline Drew's offer when her phone rang.

Without checking to see who it was, she answered it. "Hello?"

"Hey, Emma? It's me."

She just sat there as her heart clutched inside feeling as if it were about to leap out of her chest.

"It's me—Drew." He spoke again.

She played it off like she did not recognize his voice. "Oh, hey, Drew. I guess I should have called you by now. I actually was just looking at the calendar and…"

"Emma, are you coming or not?" he asked bluntly.

"Well, Drew, I really don't think I am the one you need for this project. Here's the thing, Drew, I am not the same person as I was. Anyone could give you a second opinion on colors and handle the details of remodeling. I just…"

"Em, that's bull and you know it. No soul on earth can handle these details—not these, Em. That's the unique thing about you. That's why it has to be you—everything you truly love — you love in detail, *especially* that house. Don't sit there and lie to me and say you don't because I saw you at The Grove looking out at the field of flowers — looking at the house. Your eyes always give you away, Em. We spent our entire young life planning. I can't do this unless you agree to do it with me. This project needs you. *I* need you."

After a pause, he continued as she desperately tried to keep her fresh tears muffled. "Em, your work can wait. You have already told me it could. Look, we have a past, but we also were best friends in that past. Please remember that for a moment. Remember, please."

A moment passed and still she didn't respond, so he repeated the words again. This time, in a whisper. "Remember, please. Do this for me, and I will never bother you again." He still heard nothing but silence. Then, all of the sudden, Drew said something that made her burst into laughter. "Say it, Em. Say yes."

Laughter is not what he expected but it was more than welcomed.

When her laughter subsided, she told him it reminded her of the senior skit photo they took. They laughed together and reminisced for a while. The tension began to fade. Finally, she said, "Okay, Drew Dalton, I will do this project under one condition."

"Anything. Just name it."

"I mean it, Drew. The past stays in the past. We can be friends, but only friends. Do you understand?"

"You still call all the shots, don't you?" he said with a smile she could hear over the phone. "Those are qualities you can't hide. That is who you are." He laughed and was so relived she was coming.

"Drew, I am not playing."

"Yes, ma'am," he said still laughing. "Friends only and no past. Clean slate."

"Okay, and Drew, while I am working, you will probably be at work anyway right? I won't see you much anyway."

"Yeah, that's right."

"When do we start?"

"Monday morning."

"No way. I have to clear it with work and get someone to water my plants and cancel the…"

"Oh yeah. I forgot you need at least a week to pack, and you mean dust your plants, don't you? I know you didn't inherit your mom's green thumb."

"Drew, I don't have to…"

"Emma, Emma I'm just joking. Okay, woman. Wow. Somebody needs a vacation."

"Well, I will be there on Monday of next week at…"

"Eight a.m."

"Excuse me?"

"Okay, nine."

"Really?"

"Okay. Okay. Ten a.m. and no later. Gosh you are still a pain in the *butt*, I see."

"Well, you leave my *butt* out of this. Goodbye, Drew. I will see you in a week."

"Bye, Em, and hey, Em, thanks."

"Sure," she replied adding to it with a soft, "goodbye." She hung up the phone wondering what in the world she was thinking agreeing to this.

Chapter Twelve

"Life is like music. You must know when to turn the page."
~Author Unknown

ELLA ASHBY WAS not in the shop when Emma arrived on that Sunday. It was a sunny June afternoon, and although it had been a good day to travel, Emma was relieved to have a little while to get unpacked and unwind before actually having a conversation with anyone.

Drew had called every single day that week to make sure she had not backed out on the project. However, something he said stuck with her, and she kept rehashing it in her mind. In their last phone conversation, she had gotten tired of him insinuating that she would be the type of person to back out on him without giving an explanation as to why. She thought of the way they parted that summer and got madder each time she thought about it.

Finally, she'd had enough and replied curtly to his snide comments saying, "Well, I can assure you, *Mr. Dalton*, if I were not going to follow through with a plan I made with anyone — especially a friend, then I would have the common decency to actually call and let them know."

His response lingered inside her. It was simply,

"First time for everything."

He did not say it rudely. Still, it cut straight through her. She knew he meant to hit her in the heart, and it hit hard. Why he would even think she would do something like that was beyond her. That was not at all like her. She never would, nor could she, just walk out on anyone or anything — unlike him.

Maybe it was his guilt talking. Maybe he assumed because he left her heart bleeding in her hand that August day that she would find a way to make him bleed as a payback. That must be it, but it made her so angry. Did he not know her better than that? He knew her. He knew her better than most anyone ever had, she thought. If he did not know she was incapable of doing something like that, then maybe he didn't know her at all, though.

Well, it would all be done by the end of July, so after that, her 'bird dogin" would be done, as her Daddy D would say. She never knew what that meant, but she felt it would apply in this situation. Her job would be over, and she would never have to deal with Drew Dalton ever again.

After unpacking and settling in, she remembered the box under her bed. Although she knew it was not the best idea to relive those memories, she determined there may be good photographs of the house in there. She hoped something could offer fresh inspiration and get this process going because the sooner she left Leyton, the better.

She made herself comfortable on the bed and reluctantly opened the box. The memories once again swept over her like a rushing wind. She wondered how she ever transitioned from the girl in the box to the workaholic woman she was now.

Soon, she was lost in another time as she looked at picture after picture. Cheerleading pictures, swimming at the pool with all her friends, pictures from *The Christmas Carol* play they did in the eighth grade. She really started laughing when she saw pictures of her and Jane dressed like crayons. They had always volunteered at a preschool center during the summer, and the teacher always had a creative idea that involved them wearing humiliating outfits of some sort. The pictures brought back so many happy memories. Kool-aid stands, school banquets, pep rallies, football games, all of the friends at Mazi's, and then she froze. She picked up the next picture of her and Drew at prom. Why was it still so hard?

It was her all-time favorite picture of them. His six-one frame towered over her five-one pint-sized self. They stood face-to-face with her just under his head. She looked straight up at him, and he bent down right into her face. The way he looked at her captured her heart. She smiled — so happy — so completely in love with him. They looked into one another's eyes, but his eyes spoke to her. She remembered feeling the moment as if she were there all over again.

They were on the dance floor and no longer realized anyone else was there. Even now, she had no idea if music was actually playing or not. All she remembered was feeling his heartbeat, as they were as close as they could possibly be in each other's arms. When he stopped her, he placed his free hand behind her head, and tilted her up and she stared into his eyes. They drew her like gravity into him. She saw herself in him and she felt him pouring himself over inside her. She felt, in that moment, that they'd always be together. In that one, breathtaking moment, she tried to speak, but when she opened her mouth, he placed his hand tenderly on her face, and with a single finger, he touched her lips and said in the faintest whisper of a voice, "Shhh. I just want to look at you for a minute. You're so beautiful, Em." After that, he bent down, softly kissed her, and then looked deeply into her eyes once more. He whispered, "I love you, Emma Ashby," placed her hand over his heart, and asked, "Do you feel it?"

"Hey, Emma," her mother called out. "Emma? I'm home."

She snapped back into the real world upon hearing her mom's voice.

Ella made her way to her daughter's room and stood outside the door. "Hey. You okay?"

"Oh, yeah. I was looking through some old pictures seeing if I could find some of the old house. I wanted to come up with a few ideas before tomorrow."

"Are you sure you're up to this, Em?"

"Of course, Mom. There is no reason for me not to be. It's a project for a family I love, and I'm helping an old friend. It's for one month."

"Okay," her mom said with doubt in her voice. She made her way into the room and looked directly at Emma. "Oh dear. Here we go again," she said rolling her eyes. "When you're done, let's go next door to the café and grab a bite."

"Sure. Give me a minute. I'll be there in a few. Go on without me if you want."

"Okay. I will order your regular?"

"Sounds perfect." As her mom closed the door, Emma yelled, "And…"

Her mom peeped back inside the door and said, "Don't forget the extra ice, I know." Then, she walked out again laughing.

Emma continued to sift through the box and her walk down memory lane. She and Drew had so much fun together over the years. There were pictures of her feeding him ice cream cones, school plays on the lake with their families, and the picture he took of her lying in the midst of the yellow flowers. The pictures seemed endless—Drew clowning around with the kids at church, her 'posing' on top of the Mustang, and then, him 'posing' on the Mustang making fun of her. The water gun fight picture almost got to her. She felt tears welling up and decided to concentrate on the task at hand. All she needed to do was to get in her 'Drew' state of mind the night before she was going to see him again. She finally she found the ones of the house she'd been looking for. She stuck them inside her purse and left to join her mom.

"Well, there you are," Ella said standing up to give her daughter a hug.

"Did you order yet? I am starving."

"Yeah, it'll be a few minutes, but while I was waiting I walked over to the wall and found a few pictures of the house. Mazi said you were welcome to borrow them if you would like."

"Really? That'd be great," she replied as her mom handed them to her. Then she reached into her purse to retrieve the ones she'd brought as well. "How is it that I have never noticed these before?" she asked as she spread all the pictures out before them.

As the ladies continued to sift through the pictures, Ella answered her daughter's question carefully. She paused, looked at her, and said, "Funny how some things are right in front of us, yet we never notice because we are so busy looking at everything else. The 'big picture' is made up of many smaller ones. Without the small ones, you really wouldn't have a picture at all, now would you? If someone ever asked me how they could know what their 'big picture' looked like, I would tell them to look at all the little ones, and then they'd have their answer."

While Emma was deep in that thought, Deputy Moose walked in with Darby Spenser. Emma was beginning to wonder if every day she spent in Leyton would be as drama-filled as her last trip home. She waved, and Darby and Moose waved back. Thankfully, and much to Emma's relief on many levels, Jane walked through the door just behind them and joined the Ashby women at their table.

The first word out of Jane's mouth was in a singsong tone. "Awkward."

"I'm glad I didn't have tea in my mouth because I'm pretty sure I would've spewed it all over my mom," Emma said. "So, are they a thing now, Jane?"

"Who knows? Poor Darby. Calvin is the only person she knows here, and Julie insists that Darby still help out at the store here in Leyton once a week."

"That's awful," Ella chimed in. "But Darby doesn't seem to mind too much."

"Emma, dang girl, things are always dull as dirt, and the minute you roll into town, everything turns upside down. You *do* realize that everyone in town thought you were the sole reason Drew and Darby broke up, right? You two caused quite a buzz, and from the looks of things, the summer is about to get extremely entertaining."

"Ha, Ha. Very funny, Jane. Look, people in this town live for scandal. Let 'em talk. I have nothing to hide."

Right then, the food came out. They spent the next hour batting around ideas for the house. Jane suggested a few places in Pulaski that had great pieces of antique furniture. They talked about how important it was to bring the character out in each room by enhancing what was already there. The ideas kept flowing until they were mentally exhausted from discussing the house. They decided to put it up for the night and have one more cup of coffee before calling it a night

Before they left, Jane gave them town updates. "That little angry preacher, oh my word, he really is a whack job. He got mad at sweet Lisa Jo over a funeral service. How do you get mad about what music the organist plays at a funeral?" Jane said while crunching on a chip. "Especially at Lisa? Can you believe that?" she continued. "Of course, he twisted everyone's words, and now he has the church divided right down the middle. Folks around here don't know what or who to believe anymore."

"He'll be found out. The truth about people and situations *always* has a way revealing itself," her mom said and looked at Emma.

Again, Emma was relieved for an interruption even if it was by Moose and Darby stopping at the table to say hello. They all gave a slightly awkward, yet friendly hello then Jane jumped up saying, "Well, I'd better go now if I'm going to make it to the grocery store before it closes."

Darby smiled and softly laughed. "I still can't believe there is a town left in America that actually shuts down everything but one gas station by nine p.m." Then they casually left saying goodbye.

After Jane left, Moose asked Ella to help him figure out who was in one of the pictures hanging on the wall. As they walked away, Emma realized that it was a planned meeting.

"Emma, I know this may sound strange, but I asked Calvin if he'd give me a minute to be alone with you."

"Okay. That's fine, Darby. And I was sorry to hear about you and Drew."

"Oh, no. Don't be. We just didn't have what it took, ya know? That is part of the reason I wanted to speak to you now."

"To me? Really? Darby, I hope you don't think—" she started defensively.

"Emma, listen. Let me explain. I always knew something, some part of Drew, was missing. I never could understand because no one ever filled in the blanks for me. There were just missing pieces of his life, and he just acted as if they weren't ever there. I knew you two grew up together and were great friends that turned into a 'thing' later in high school, but I had no idea the depth of the relationship.

"In April, the first time I saw him look at you at the reception, I knew instantly that you were his missing part. The night we broke off the engagement, he promised me he would talk to you, but as deep as his denial went, I bet he hasn't yet. Whatever you think or believe, well, just be open to him, if he should choose to finally talk to you about it. I know what I know. The man is crazy in love with you. That's rare, so don't walk away unless you're sure it's the right thing."

"Darby, I don't—"

"Emma, he still has your picture in a frame under his bed. In the picture, you are lying in a field of flowers by the cabin, I believe."

Tears formed in Emma's eyes as she felt the weight of Darby's words. She was afraid to feel them because she knew there would be no way to hide her feelings once they were exposed. She quickly reminded herself that he hadn't wanted her, and she started to share that with Darby, but she really just wanted the conversation to end, so she didn't.

"Trust me. He is still in love with you, and I'm okay with that. At first, I wasn't, but I finally realized what I told him was true. The night I left, I told him that *I* wanted to be someone's Emma. When somebody isn't in love with you back, there is no way it's real love. I realized my other half was still out there looking for me, and I needed to try, at the very least, to meet him half way. If two people are meant to be, they always find their way to one another, or sometimes *back to* one another. I really do believe that, Emma. So see, I didn't have that forever kind of love for Drew after all, and that's what I want. Don't you?"

Emma tried to comprehend Darby's words, but Darby interrupted her thoughts by speaking once again.

"And Emma, watch out for Julie. She *really, really* hates you. It's like she has a vendetta against you — some mission to ruin your life."

"Now there's a news flash," Emma said jokingly.

"I am serious. Don't trust her."

A little shaken by her words once again, Emma said. "Okay. Thanks for the warning. You didn't have to tell me any of this, you know."

"Actually, I did. You need to know the truth, and if I, in any way, can help you find it, I had to try."

"Well, thanks. I think you are an incredible person, Darby. You were engaged to this guy, and now you are professing his love for me *for* him. That's unheard of — not that I believe that you're right, but I do believe that *you* believe he does, and that means a lot to me. Thank you."

"There was no choice. You had to know. You truly 'fit' together. I just hope you two discover it soon, before it's too late. It seems like everybody around here knows that you are stronger and better together than you will ever be apart, except maybe Julie."

Emma touched Darby's hand, looked in her eyes, and sincerely thanked her again. Then it was Emma's turn, and she asked a few questions about Darby and Calvin. Emma was thrilled to see Darby's eyes sparkle when she answered her questions.

The last thing Darby said that stayed with Emma the most was, "Do you know how good it feels to look into someone's eyes and see *yourself* for a change?"

The question resonated throughout Emma's body. She knew just what Darby was saying. She had always seen herself in Drew's eyes.

About that time, her mom and Moose returned to the table.

"Well, Miss Darby, I had better take you to your car so I can get myself back to work. Hope I will see you around, Emma."

"Oh, the chances are likely, Moose. I will be here for

most of the summer it looks like."

"Great. Well, we'd better get going. You ladies have a good evening. Goodnight."

The ladies said goodnight, and as they started leaving, Emma called out, "Hey, Darby. Thanks again for everything."

Her reply was, "The best way to thank me is don't forget all that I said." Then with her sweet smile, she said, "Well, goodnight."

Back at the shop, Emma filled her mom in on all that Darby shared. Mama El had to voice her opinion, agreeing with Darby. They talked some, but Emma was exhausted and needed sleep. The house was going to be a challenge, but she knew her greatest challenge, for sure, was Drew.

As she collapsed onto her bed, memories of her and Drew continued to play inside her heart until she fell asleep. She met the one and only man she'd ever loved.

Chapter Thirteen

"All our dreams can come true if we have the courage to pursue them."
~Walt Disney

Emma was so proud of herself for pulling up at The Point at 9:45 am. Of course, she had to wake up at the crack of dawn to make it on time, but no one needed to know that. Dressed in old jeans, work boots, and a T-shirt with a large cup of black coffee in her hand, she carried her clipboard in her other hand, ready for the day. Drew's car was out front so she braced herself for their early morning encounter. Stepping inside, she heard the sounds of the construction workers throughout the house. The butterflies in her stomach quickly turned into bats as she waited on Drew to appear.

Finally, she called out, "Drew? Hey, it's me — Emma. I'm here."

When he walked into the room, their eyes locked. She could feel the butterflies inside her stirring as they stood in the very room where they had spent a magical night together long ago. He glanced down at his watch, looked back at her, and smiled that smile still able to grab her heart.

Jokingly, he said, "Well, well, well. Look who is

early. Well, early for 'Emma Time' anyway."

"Good morning to you too, *funny man*," she sarcastically joked back.

"So, Mr. Boss Man, where do we start?"

"Oh, so I *finally* actually get to be the boss? Nice."

"Well, today anyway." She laughed. "But don't count on it for long."

"Why don't we walk through the entire house and take a look and go from there? I also want to walk over some things outside with you."

She nodded in agreement and walked through a wall of plastic while following his lead.

As she came out on the other side, he waved out his hands saying, "The first stop…"

Her eyes came alive as if someone reached inside her and flipped a switch. "Drew. The staircase…" She cheered as she headed toward it. "Is it ready? Is it okay to walk up?"

She lit up just like the little girl from long ago. She had been so full of wonder and perfectly aware of the unseen magic all around her. Putting his hand out Drew replied, "Ladies first."

The staircase began in the entrance hall and curved around in a perfect U shape until reaching the second floor great room. It was as lovely as she always dreamed it would be. She couldn't believe the detail in the architecture. It all seemed so mystic, so alluring as it drew you right into its very essence.

They talked briefly and were both in agreement about leaving the original, ornate woodwork if at all salvageable. There were five rooms off the second floor great room and just before her was the balcony. She looked at Drew once again as the excitement almost took her breath away. "Is it safe?"

"Knock yourself out," he replied giving her a quick wink.

Emma walked out onto the balcony, looking down on the magnolia and old oak trees. Taking a deep, cleansing breath, contentment fell upon her. It was as wonderful as she always thought it would be. Memories of the days when she imagined this space was her kingdom came rushing back.

From behind her, she felt Drew, but she had no idea how he was looking at her. Did he feel what she was feeling too? She ached from wanting him to hold her so badly. She tried to talk herself out her thoughts, but her heart kept overruling her head. She wanted him to walk up behind her, slip his arms around her, and kiss her more than anything at the moment. A sudden crash from downstairs caused both of them to break from the moment and rush back downstairs.

They were glad to know it was only a sawhorse that had accidentally been tangled up in an extension cord and fallen over with a few coffee cups on top of it. The echo throughout the house made everything seem louder since no furniture was there to buffer or absorb the sound. Since everything was okay, they resumed the tour.

Off to the right and left of the entrance hall were rounded archways that led to the three large rooms on each side. On the left portion, it had an additional sunroom with a curved, glass bay window encasing the east porch. It was extraordinary and quite spacious. Emma knew it had great potential to be her favorite.

There was only a small kitchen inside the house because the main kitchen was just outside. During the time when the house was originally built, in the 1800s, the kitchen was not part of the home's interior. The kitchen was not even connected to the house at all. It was in the backyard attached by a walkway and was referred to as the 'cook house.' Emma liked that and said it added a great deal of charm to the atmosphere and made a note of that as well.

After taking a few pictures throughout the house, they went outside by way of the front double doors.

"Drew, this front porch is still as big as I remembered." Again, memories raced through both of their minds, but for now, they chose to discuss a few early ones.

"Em, we were crazy little kids, ya know? Kids don't play like we did anymore, do they?"

"Drew, I don't think normal kids played the way we did back then, but we had a *ton* of fun. Remember all the plays we performed for no one—or anyone that would come?"

"Remember? How could I forget all the things you made me do. You know, you still aren't off the hook for making me wear those tights the time you just had to make me be Peter Pan."

"You know you loved it."

She was having a conversation but steadily making notes as they walked along. She saw the magnolia tree from the bottom now instead of the top. "How long has this magnolia been here, Drew? Do you know?"

"Actually, I *do* know the answer to that. My great, great grandfather, Sinclair Hastings, moved into this house in the late 1800s, but my great grandfather, Sinclair Hastings II, actually planted *two* trees here in 1938, the year he and my great grandmother moved in here. He had them sent in from Mobile, AL, as a gift for her. Undoubtedly, he adored his wife, according to my mom. He wanted to do something that would symbolize his great love for her and would grow like the love they shared had."

"I love that, Drew," she replied as she stood mesmerized by the story. "How romantic. I can't believe I never heard that story before."

"I just heard it for the first time last year. Mom knew I was itching to start the renovations so she told me all she could remember. Undoubtedly, it was rare to see a magnolia around this area so it made the gift even that more special."

"You said he planted two?" she asked curiously looking around. "So what happened to the other one?"

"Mom said the other one was struck by lightning or hit by a tornado or something. I can't remember, but it was long before our time here. Actually, what fascinated me was what she told me about the root system they shared. They grew together, so actually, even though one tree is gone, the other lives on inside the other — kinda neat bit of trivia don't ya think?"

"Oh my word. That's incredible." She rubbed her arms and shivered saying, " Look. I have goose bumps. Anything else I don't know about this place?"

"Oh yeah, out back, down about forty yards or so from the barn, you will never believe what they found."

"You mean to tell me there is something on the premises we didn't uncover growing up?"

"Would you believe they found an abandoned well?"

"Another one? I thought the gazebo surrounded the only well on the property, hence the old 'well house'."

"Me too, but a few weeks ago, when the appraiser came out, he came across it. Mom almost collapsed on the spot thinking about how we played out here almost every day and never fell in." He walked around picking up a few scrap pieces of wood that were lying on the ground. "It is scary now that you think about it."

"Really? I still can't believe we never found it."

"It was a miracle he found it, but it had rained a great deal before he came out that day, and there was a distinct depression in the ground that made it visible. It was covered by an old, rotting gate door, and my parents said they thought it was just old wood like that in the old gazebo we found."

He walked back over to stand beside her again. "Someone is coming to seal it in a few weeks or so. The guy is busy on another job but said he'd get to it as soon as possible, although it may be mid-July before he can make it out here. Anyway, it's marked with yellow caution tape, as you'll see. Actually, not even you could miss it," he remarked with a smirk. She knew he was remembering how oblivious she was about certain things. "I know it's out of the way, but you know how people will be starting to poke and prod around to see what progress we are making here," he quickly added, "on the house, you know."

Pretending to not even be fazed by his remark, she made a few more notes and then said, "I guess this is about it?"

"Yeah, this is pretty much it."

"So, now what exactly should we do next?"

"Well, we need to sit down and decide the best use for the house, I think. Then that will help set the use for each room." He looked at her again; she thought he was about to say more but he didn't. Instead, he shifted his body a bit and added, "That is what I was thinking anyway. Sound like a plan to you?"

Pretending to stare at her notes, she was really wondering just how much time she'd have to spend with him, and while still looking at her paper, she said, "Sounds good to me."

"Why don't we go to Mazi's, grab some lunch, and then get on it?"

"Okay, but you are buying."

Making a bowing gesture he said playfully, "Why of course, my lady."

They walked around the corner and looked at their choices of transportation. He looked at Emma and asked, "Jeep or Mustang?"

She smiled her sassy, playful smile and said, "Do you even have to ask? First one there gets to drive!" she exclaimed as she got a running start.

Since he was twice her size, he took a few steps and jumped over into the driver's side of the convertible Mustang. She knew she wouldn't get to drive and really didn't want to today anyway. With the top of the car down, she just wanted to let the wind rush all over her again, like when she was younger and didn't have a care. She turned the music up and enjoyed being in the Mustang with her old friend again.

They were already the talk of the week according to Jane, ranking in at second place because the crazy preacher still held the number one spot. The last thing she needed was everyone seeing her drive his car. However, halfway there, she spied his cowboy hat on the back seat, and she put it on. She made her mind up that if they were going to talk, she might as well not disappoint and really work this.

They walked into the café still laughing and singing. When they looked up, they saw the entire place staring at them. She still had on his hat, and he still had his shades on. Their hair was windblown, and they simply looked at each other and burst out laughing.

He leaned down and whispered, "This is gonna be fun."

She truly laughed from deep within herself, and it felt so free, so natural. They took a booth that looked directly at "The Wall" and realized they were sitting just where they always sat growing up. They reminisced more about the years they shared together, being very careful to stop before getting too deep into their memories as a couple. Being together seemed natural to them, so right.

The young girl that came to take the order looked confused seeing Drew with someone other than Darby. She was really taken back when he asked Emma if he could order for her just to see if he still could remember what she always ordered. Of course, she said yes.

"I will have a club sandwich on white and an order of onion rings, and *she'll* have a chicken salad sandwich on wheat with a pickle on the side."

"Impressive, Mr. Boss Man."

The waitress then asked, "And to drink?"

"I will have a large Coke, and she'll have a large unsweetened tea with extra ice."

The waitress left with their menus that they never even looked at, and Emma spoke up saying, "I really can't believe you can remember that."

Then his gaze locked onto hers and he said, "I

remember everything about you, Em."

Thankfully, their drinks arrived, which broke the look they could not seem to let go of, and it was an open door to change the subject back to work.

"So Drew, do you have anything in mind for the way you want to market the house? What will its function be?"

"Well, that's just it. It could be so many things. My first thought was a bed and breakfast, but I don't plan on living there and there is no way I want anyone else to either."

"Any other thoughts in that head of yours?" she asked curiously.

"It could be another place to host events and dinners, but that was the entire point of Hastings Hall. I thought of a museum of sorts. You know, some place for local memorabilia to be displayed by the townspeople—and one more idea, but it is a stretch of imagination."

"Hey, it's me, remember? Us. Imagination is what 'we' do best. So whatcha got?"

The food arrived and just as the waitress walked away, he said, "Okay, but don't laugh at me."

"Okay," she said and took a bite out of her pickle.

"What if it were a place where the community could perform? The front could even be used as a stage for concerts and community theatre. And if it became big enough, we could book acts from other places to coincide with things like the July 4th celebration in the community, or the Flywheel, or Christmas—things that we all celebrate together. We could have a few rooms upstairs for accommodations for special guests only. Then, we could renovate the kitchen out back and it could always serve as a functioning tearoom opened

THE Point

daily to the public and booked by reservation only at night. It would have to be on a small scale because of limited space, but if someone needed more space, that is what the Hall is for."

When he stopped talking, she just sat there until he finally said somewhat sheepishly, "So, is it stupid? Tell the truth. I can take it."

"I absolutely love it!" she exclaimed. "One problem though, the porch is large enough for a few things but not for something like community theater productions. Let's think about an alternative for that, but I love this vision." She took another bite out of her pickle and with genuine excitement in her eyes said, "This is perfect, Drew."

"Really? Good." He was elated at her response. "I knew if anyone would get the performing part of it, you would. This way, it could have multi purposes, and each would benefit the community. It's a win-win."

"When the time comes," she asked, "How will you promote it?"

"Well, see, I happen to know this incredibly talented lady who is a brilliant advertising agent, and I bet she will help guide us in the direction we should go." He flashed that smile again at her.

She smiled back saying, "Yeah, I hear she rocks."

Laughing, they clicked their glasses together and said, "Cheers."

Drew paid their tab, but as they were leaving, they came face to face with Julie and his mom. Mrs. Liza immediately flung her arms around Emma saying, "Emma, honey, I am so glad you agreed to help Drew with the house. No one loves that old place the way you two always have."

"I am excited to be helping him," Emma said hugging her back. Then she reluctantly said, "Hello, Julie."

"Oh, hello," was Julie's only response. The coolness in Julie's tone matched her gaze upon Emma when she asked, "And how long will you be here?"

Drew and Liza looked at her in shock at her attitude, so Julie altered her demeanor. "Of course, I want us to be sure and have some girl time."

"Oh, I'll be here about a month or maybe a little more," Emma replied. Emma clearly saw through Julie's façade.

"Well, I will look you up soon so we can catch up."

"Of course," Emma said.

With that, Drew placed his hand on Emma's back and announced that they needed to be heading back. They said goodbye and got into the Mustang again. This time, the mood had changed. What could have Emma possibly done to make Julie this angry? She hated her, it seemed. Emma's thoughts hovered a minute about the warning Darby had given her, but there was no way she was sharing with Drew that Darby came to see her. He would want to know what she said, and there was no way under the Tennessee sun she was revealing that to him. Nope, she had work to do, and work was what she did best. One month, then she'd be gone. Drew even cranked up the Eagles and they listened to Hotel California and the wind on the drive back.

As they pulled into the drive, Drew tried to find words to approach the topic of Julie. "I am so sorry about Julie, Em. I don't know what her problem is."

"No, it's okay. She's been this way for some time

now."

"No, it's *not* okay, and I don't remember her being this bad. Anyway, I am sorry. She never comes out to the house, so unless you see her in town, she shouldn't be around you. She lives in Pulaski, but since she's opening the second store here, she stays over a lot — especially with Benji out of school for the summer. She has such a great heart. I have never seen her be quite this rude before — even to you."

"Well, I can handle her. Besides, I am used to it by now. The fact that I am working with you, no doubt, has her upset more than usual considering how she feels toward me."

"Well, if she becomes a problem, just say the word, but if I know my mom, she is giving her an earful about now." They got out of the car and discussed a few last minute details before saying goodbye. As he turned and walked toward the house, he looked back and said, "Emma, thanks for coming."

"Thanks for asking, and thanks again for lunch," she said as she waved goodbye.

"I'll call you later."

"Okay. Bye."

"Goodbye."

As she drove away, she painfully began to realize she could no longer neatly place him in and out of the box she kept him in. This was not a memory to be tucked away, this was really happening now. The realness of him was stronger than ever, but if he had wanted her and had really loved her, she would have heard from him in the past seven years. She knew if she could keep him from attacking any more of her senses she could possibly survive the month without her heart overtaking her. The last thing she wanted was for him to think she was some pathetic woman that was still hopelessly in love with him—or in love with the man he *used* to be anyway. Distance—she needed to remember distance. She had to do her work without him and made a mental note to enforce that, starting tomorrow.

Chapter Fourteen

"Once you put the pieces back together, even though you may
Look intact, you are never quite the same as you were before the fall."
~Jodi Picoult

EMMA ARRIVED AT The Point about nine a.m. She had a few more details to settle in her mind before she spoke with the contractor. She had rehearsed how she would handle Drew if he tried to hang out at the house or spend too much personal time with her. She thought she'd say something like, "Drew, there is a lot of work to do, and I only have a small window of time, so I think we could get more done if we actually worked separately then checked in with each other. There is no reason we have to do this side by side now that we have focused on the goal and outcome."

Who was she kidding? She was everything but focused. She had allowed her heart to become too involved and had relived the heartbreak all over again. She had played the familiar game of finding her scattered pieces and putting them back together again and hoping they were a little more firmly placed this time. She hoped it worked because every time she had seen him in the past, she fell into his eyes all over again.

About an hour after she'd been there, Drew drove up. He was in his truck, which was odd. She said aloud to herself, "Well Em, let's try and put the plan into action right now shall we?"

"Knock, knock," he said as he walked in the door. She knew this was going to be hard because she felt him getting closer with every step, and he wasn't even in the same room with her yet.

He stood in the door frame looking gorgeous, smelling *almost* as good as he looked in his perfect fitting jeans, white button up shirt, and cowboy boots. She was too far gone to think of a word, so all she could come up with was, "Hey."

Afraid her blotches were betraying her emotion, she forced herself to look the other direction. How could she resist this? What was wrong with her? She was trying to put at least one sentence together before he came any closer all the while thinking how ridiculous this all was when thankfully, he spoke again.

"Good morning. Look who's up and running early this morning."

"What do you need, Drew?" she asked acting as if she were preoccupied with work.

"Um, a 'Good to see you too, Drew' or just a 'Good Morning, Drew' with eye contact or, how about 'Man, you're looking sexier than *ever* this morning, Drew?' I personally like that one the best," he said with a lethal smile.

She snapped rudely back saying, "Drew, what do you need? I am busy." Just as he opened his mouth to answer, she said, knowing it was now or never, "No, wait a minute. I have something I have to say, so hear me out." She stood up in a professional manner and continued. "You said this would be strictly business and nothing more. We were close, yes, years ago. Then we were a couple. Now, we aren't. I am here on behalf of our past and my love for your family, period. No more, no less. I am here because you asked me to help build our memories, but that is all *we* are now. We are just a memory, Drew. So, you work, wherever you work, and I will work here. Okay? And that means no hanging out, no eating lunch, none of that. Understood?"

A stunned, hurt Drew stood blankly staring at her. "Where did this come from, Em? I thought we were good. I did not..." He searched for words, but none seemed appropriate.

"And don't call me Em. I am not your EM anymore, Drew," she said biting back. Then calmer, she continued, "You didn't do anything. I just don't think it looks good, and in a month, our lives resume back the way they were. It's best this way."

He responded heatedly, "Oh yeah, I know how much you worship that 'life' of yours." Then he said coldly, "You know, looks like you chose the right one when you chose your career."

"What are you talking about?"

Visibly trying to calm down a notch, Drew answered, "Look, Em. *Sorry.* Emma, I have no intention of being up under you or making up excuses to see or be with you. You made your mind up long ago."

Even though she tried to interrupt, he held his hand up and kept talking. "And not that it is any of your business, but I have a meeting in Pulaski with some investors in my company after work today, so don't flatter yourself thinking I dressed up for you."

"I just thought," Emma softly spoke.

"Well, you 'thought' wrong didn't you?" he asked.

She was sitting on the floor and feeling like a fool. While fighting the urge not to cry, she was finally able to say, "You're right. I am sorry. We chose our path a long time ago. Sorry. I was out of line. The past is past, and it is what it is. So I will get busy, and if I have a question, I will call you."

"Deal. Well, I will leave you to it then. Goodbye, *Emma*."

"Bye," she said with a half wave.

She winced as she heard the door slam then watched him drive down the hill. She could no longer hold the tears in. She caved. She cried for what was, what was no longer, and what would never be. Her heart was breaking in places she had not even been aware she even had; this was a new level of fresh pain. She realized that not only was she still in love with him but she would never really be able to love anyone else the way she loved him. She dropped her papers and ducked her head between her legs and arms while the rest of her shattered.

DRIVING DOWN THE hill, Drew felt the sting of tears in his eyes and reached to push them away. He was thankful for the hour drive ahead of him because he had to regroup. He didn't have to dress up to meet with these guys. They were old college buddies, and this was just a lunch to catch up about the company they had invested in long ago. He really was going because Julie needed some things moved to the Leyton store. John had enough to deal with launching the second store, so the least Drew could do was transport boxes.

He remembered how angry Julie had gotten at

Emma the summer they broke up. He thought of how rude Julie had been to Emma at the café the day before, too. She had seen him cry as if someone died the day Emma left. He shut down, and he died a little more every day it seemed. His sister knew, even now, that he was not the same as before. Jules had been so wonderful, and he wouldn't know what he'd have done without having her, John, and Benji to keep him occupied. Even introducing him to Darby was her way of taking care of him.

She warned him about asking Emma to help, but he thought it would be okay — maybe even thought, deep down, they would have another shot, but he was wrong. He made a mental note to thank Jules and tell her how much he loved her and that he'd never doubt her again. Before that, for the next hour, he was going to explain to his heart that Emma was not coming back — no matter how badly it had anxiously been waiting for her return. It was time to let her go, and maybe this time, between his words and the cleansing of his tears, his heart would listen. His Emma was not really *his* after all.

When Drew pulled up to the store, John came over to Drew and shook his hand saying, "I appreciate this, man. We have got to get this merchandise moved out because in two weeks, your sister and I are going to market in New York."

"Really? I'm sorry, man. That sounds awful."

John laughed and said, "No, it's wonderful. I really

don't mind but I hate leaving, Benji. Although, he's so happy he gets to spend the weekend with his Gran and Daddy D, but he's the most excited to hang with his Uncle Drew."

"I could use some company—don't know how much good I'll be though."

Looking a bit concerned John asked, "You okay, man?"

"Oh yeah — just projects — deadlines, you know how it is — especially dealing with women — one in particular."

"Speaking of women, can I ask you a personal question, Drew?"

He braced himself for the Emma topic to come up next, and was glad he had dealt with that on the drive over because he sure didn't want to let on to anyone what was going on inside him. "Sure."

"Are you okay, really? You know, with Darby and Calvin spending so much time together?"

What a relief, he thought. "I am fine, really. I'm glad for both of them. Darby is an incredible woman, and Moose—you know he is one of my best friends. I think they are a great idea."

"Really?" he asked again. "I know Calvin is my brother, but you are like my brother too, man. You know you can tell me if you're really not okay with them."

"I swear to you, I am fine. Really."

Then John opened the door of the store and they walked inside. "So, what about Emma?"

There was the million-dollar question everyone wanted to ask. "Well, as you know, Emma is working with me on a project. In a month, it'll be done, and she'll leave — the end," he said emotionless.

"Any chance she may stay?"

"Not a chance in hell," he stated frankly. "She'll leave. That's what Emma does best."

Julie walked up in time to hear his comment and said, "That's good to hear, and don't you forget that, little brother." She said hugging him with a smile then walked over to her husband and leaned over giving him a peck on his cheek and saying, "Hey, Sweetheart."

"Hey, Jules," John responded back affectionately.

"Drew, thank you so much for picking this up for me. It's mainly clothes, but there are a few shoes in there, too. Oh, that reminds me, Darby needed some office supplies. I'll be right back." She scooted off to the back again.

"It's good to see her so excited," John said. "She loves this store, and she's in her element expanding like this."

"It's good to see you all happy. She really loves you, John," Drew said enviously.

"It's a good thing because I am kind of in love with her, too." He winked as she came back.

"Here is one box of supplies, but there is one more under my desk. John, could you get it for me, please?" She gave him a quick kiss. "And can you load it up for me?" she asked with a giggle.

"Sure, honey," he said as he walked to the back.

"Drew, are you okay? You look, I don't know… down I guess."

"I am fine, Jules. Stop worrying about me."

"How can I with that woman who broke my little brother's heart back in town? What in this world were you thinking asking her back after all this time?"

"Julie, I love that you love me so much, and thanks for always having my best interest at heart, but really, I'm okay. Besides, Emma and I decided, actually *she* did, that it's best not to even work together on this renovation. So, no need to worry your pretty little head." He kissed her on her cheek.

"Well, good. I do love you, dear brother, but I have to run. Benji's swimming lesson is over in five minutes. See you later, and thanks again," she said running out the door.

John came back in, handed the box to Drew, and thanked him again as well. "Well, tell Darby hello, and if she sees anything else that the store needs, let us know, and hey, ask her before she heads back tonight if she'd run by Petals and pick up the flowers I ordered. I'm taking Julie out to dinner to celebrate the new store opening, and she loves flowers. Do you mind?"

Drew shook his head then John's hand saying, "Will do."

Drew met his friends for a quick lunch and update on the business, and then headed back to Leyton. He turned on a country radio station because he never listened to country music with Emma. She was not a huge fan of country. As soon as the song ended, the Krispie Kritter commercial she wrote came on. He turned the radio off and drove home in silence.

No matter what he tried, or how hard he tried, there was just no shaking Emma. She was his every other thought, lingering just on the edge of him at all times. Who was he kidding? He knew the only woman he'd ever really love was Emma — even if she did not love him. She was an addiction that seemed impossible for him to break. His short-term goal was just to survive the month with a shred of anything that still may resemble his heart. Then he would deal with the fallout, but for now, he just had to give the performance of his life. Hopefully, he could convince everyone more than he could convince himself that he really didn't love Emma Ashby anymore.

After arriving back in Leyton, he dropped the boxes off at The Knit Whit first. He was glad to see Moose there because he needed help unloading the merchandise. He was thankful the station let him come in later because the short trip had helped clear his head.

He relayed the messages to Darby from Julie and then asked about picking the flowers up for John before she headed back to Pulaski. He told her he called ahead so it should just be a matter of picking them up.

"Sure, I'll be happy to pick them up, and Drew, thanks for still being my friend," Darby said smiling.

"Darby, you will always be my friend." He smiled as he playfully winked. "And for the record, I really like you with my boy Moose."

As Moose walked back into the store, she smiled at Drew for saying that. Then Drew noticed how Darby brightened up when she looked at Moose. That made him feel better knowing she was okay and happy. At least he didn't have to worry about that. He said his goodbyes to the both of them and was on his way. Calvin headed out too.

Darby was thankful for the chance to speak to Drew and make sure they were friends. She hated that he looked so stressed, but she had done all she could by talking to both him and Emma. The rest was up to them.

She smiled thinking of Calvin. It was like she'd known him a lifetime. She was so glad Drew was comfortable with it because now she felt she could accept Julie's offer to manage the Leyton store permanently. With Benji, it was best that Julie and John remain in Pulaski for now. Still in a blissful state, she decided to roll her sleeves up and get back to work. She had a ton of new merchandise to get out that Drew had just delivered.

She began unpacking and realized she needed to be itemizing this new inventory so she could plug it into the computer later. She saw a box on the top of the stack marked office supplies. She hoped to find what she needed inside without having to stop and walk all the way to the back room.

She was so happy Julie remembered to pack extra tags because she had forgotten to ask her for them and knew she was getting low. Just as she reached down to get a pencil out, she remembered the ink cartridges and panicked when she didn't see them. Then, much to her relief, she saw a second box Drew had brought in just beside it and assumed it was what she needed. However, she realized it was just a bunch of old junk with Drew's name on it. It must have been in storage there. It looked like memorabilia of some sort. So, she wrote down on her to do list "Get ink cartridges" and "Take Drew his box back."

After work, she stopped by to pick up the flowers

John had ordered and saw Emma with paper spread all over the front room of the shop. She was meticulously going over the details as if she were in another world. Darby stepped over to say hello.

"Hey, Emma." She waved.

"Oh, hey, Darby. How are you?" she asked as she stood and stretched.

"I'm sorry, I didn't mean to bother you. Please, keep on working. I'm just about to—"

"Oh no, thank you. I get lost in work of any kind. It's my hobby, I'm afraid." She laughed. "That is pitiful, isn't it? I know. I have got to get a life. Would you like some coffee? I just made a fresh pot."

"I would love to visit, but I promised John I would get the flowers he ordered for Julie to him before their date tonight."

"He is a great guy, how he loves 'Franken Julie' is beyond me though."

"She is really a nice person, Emma. She's kind hearted, really — except with you, that is. I'm genuinely touched how she helps people in town — especially with the big brother/big sister program. She's one of the biggest supporters of the group and was even recognized at their annual banquet last year. She loves John Scott with all her heart and adores that little boy. Don't get me wrong, she is overboard crazy about Drew for sure, but except for you, I have never seen her act unbecomingly to anyone. It's not in your head, though. She really doesn't like you at all."

That made no sense to Emma. She had replayed her memories of Julie trying to remember *anything* that could have triggered this strong hatred, but she always just came up empty.

"You know, hearing you say that, I don't know if that makes me happy or sad."

"I'm sorry. It is just plain strange for me, and I can only imagine how difficult all this is for you," Darby said.

Changing the subject, Emma asked about the store and when she thought it would open. She was glad to hear Darby would be running the store because no matter what Darby said, Emma knew Julie had a dark side, and Leyton didn't deserve her full time. After a few minutes, Darby looked at her watch.

"Well, as much as I'd love to visit, I have to get these flowers to John."

"Sure. Hey, Darby, would you like to have lunch sometime?"

Smiling as usual, she said, "Yes. I'd like that."

"Great. Call you next week?"

"Sure."

"Okay. Be careful driving back. Talk to you later."

"Okay, goodbye, Emma."

EMMA SMILED HER first real smile all day. She really liked Darby, and on some level, she was glad to hear Julie wasn't a monster, but it disturbed her greatly that she hated her so much. It was almost creepy.

After a quick visit and run through of the day with her mom, she got some pictures out that she had taken of the land behind the house. She picked up a few more then decided to stop for the day after taking a break to refresh her coffee. She walked upstairs to her room and decided to sit out on the balcony for a while. She leaned back looking at the stars wondering how many nights she and Drew sat doing that together. She breathed in the summer night air and smiled. About that time, her cell rang, and seeing it was Jane, Emma went back inside because she had too much to share and certainly didn't want to risk anyone overhearing this loaded conversation.

As her French doors closed behind Emma, Drew made his way out onto his balcony. He looked over where Emma had been standing. He whispered softly to himself, "Goodnight, Em. Find me in your dreams."

Chapter Fifteen

"If you don't risk anything—you risk even more."
~Erica Zong

A few weeks passed, and Emma had kept her distance from Drew. However, this afternoon, she knew there were things she had to discuss with him.

She was happy to be meeting Alec Gresham for lunch. It had been a while since she'd seen him, and she needed a break from her deranged life. Even if it was only for an hour or so, it was better than nothing. A distraction in any form would be welcome. They decided to meet at Barney's Grill across town for lunch because it was more secluded. Barney's was not as open as the café, so the atmosphere lent itself to more private conversation. She knew if he came all the way to see her for a weekend, there was a good reason. Besides, she had to break the cycle of seeing the same people over and over again. She needed some Alec time because he would let her melt down without analyzing it the way the rest of her world would.

At twelve o'clock sharp, she walked in the front door where her friend was waiting on her. He gave her a big hug and told her hello. The hostess seated them, took their drink order, and left them. They chatted briefly until their drinks came, and then they ordered lunch.

"Can I just tell you how *fabulous* it is to see you? I have missed you, you pest," Emma chided playfully. She was grateful to him, more than he could ever know, on his impeccable timing, but this spontaneity was very unlike him and she wanted to know why. They had the short version of catch up and then she came right to the point.

"Okay, now. What in the *world* is going on? Why did you drive all this way just to see me? Spill."

"Can I not come to see my best friend without having to have a reason?"

"You don't fool me. Spit it out." She smiled but meant it. She was so glad to be on the other end of a confession for once.

"Okay, here's the thing. I am pretty sure, no, I *am* sure that I am completely and totally in love with Jane," he said it quickly and took a deep breath. "There. I finally said it out loud — and to you."

Emma was not surprised and was thrilled, but she felt a twinge inside her that she didn't understand. "And I am surprised, why?"

"I am serious, Emma. I love her. *Really* love her."

"I think it's great, but why are you telling me, Don Juan, and not Jane?"

"Because for one thing, I am terrified she'll think I am nuts and have nothing more to do with me."

"And, the second?"

"You, Emma."

"Me? What do I have to do with this?"

"Well, you know we have a past. Jane always has felt a little strange because of it and thinks she's breaking some sacred code girls have about not sharing men or something."

"I told her a long time ago that was ridiculous and gave her my blessing."

"I know, but it still feels strange. Maybe I feel strange too, Emma. Is it really okay? I don't want to come between two old friends or do anything to ever ruin our friendship. You are special to me. You know you are one of the best friends I have ever had, and the best girl I *never* had."

"What are you talking about, 'never had,' silly man?"

"I never had you, Emma. Drew is the only one who has ever had your heart. Drew still has it, too. You *do* know that, right? I tried, God only knows how hard I tried to win you over, but I knew before we ever even tried that you had no heart to give me.

"Remember, I watched you lose your mind after your breakup. I saw the life inside you leak out, literally, until the you I first met was no longer living behind your eyes. That version of you ceased to exist. I knew I was just a filler of your time, and that was okay, but we both knew a relationship had to have more than that.

"Anyway, your friendship means everything to me. I respect you far too much to confess the truth to Jane without making sure you were really okay with it — and that you thought I was worthy of her."

"Of course I do, Alec. You know, I don't think I could have made it through the past years without you, and I never really thanked you for that. Thanks, Alec. I think Jane will be the *luckiest* to have you. You deserve someone that will love you with every part of them. I *am* sorry I couldn't give that to you."

"Emma, you gave me the greatest gift — your friendship, and if it had worked out differently between the two of us, I would have missed out on Jane. I really do love her, Emma."

"Yeah," laughing she said, "I got that." Then holding her glass of tea up, she proposed a toast. "To you and Jane." They drank to that. "You have my blessings, and may all your dreams come true."

The food arrived, and he caught Emma up on office news and a few business details, but then he started in on her. "So, my friend, we've talked circles around you and your life, so now it's your turn."

"Me?" she asked trying to avoid the subject.

"Yeah, you." He hesitated little before proceeding. "What about your dreams coming true?"

With a distant, faraway look in her eyes, she answered solemnly, "Alec, somewhere along the way, I just gave up on the dream thing. Ya know, sometimes, you just have to know when to walk away."

"Emma, don't give me that crap. I know you are not going to sit there and tell me that the love of your life lives next freakin' door and you have nothing to say — not to mention he is the only reason you are here to begin with."

She was taken aback but felt resigned not to argue the point anymore. She began saying "Well, really, there's nothing to…"

Until he softly touched her hand, looked into her eyes, and said, "Emma, it's me. Please, talk to me. Don't leave it all inside this time. You have got to stop running — stop hiding."

"I always keep coming back to the same thing every time. If he had really loved me, he had seven long years to come get me and tell me, but guess what? He didn't, Alec, and then there's Julie…"

Interrupting, Alec started in with, "Oh no. What *fresh* hell has she stirred up this time?"

"Well, that's just it — she seems wonderful to everyone *except* me. I don't get why she hates me so much. Even Darby says so…"

"Darby? That's right, you and Darby are buddies now."

"I really like her. How twisted is that? Darby is with Moose now, you and Jane, and Darby and Drew, you and me…" she laughed and added, "We sure are a screwed up bunch, aren't we?"

"Darby and Moose are really hitting it off?"

"Seems like it. She really is great. Well, anyway, about Julie, she has just been too strange. Hateful to me, but to everyone else, she's just Ms. Innocent. She even asked me to lunch a few weeks ago when everyone was around. I knew she wouldn't follow through with it. I can't put my finger on it, but she has a problem with me, clearly. One day, maybe I'll figure it out."

"Well, she is a strange one, I'll say, but Julie or no Julie, it's your turn to be honest. Take a risk and tell Drew the truth. If you can't keep working under these conditions, tell him, but tell him the truth. Tell him today. Life is way too short, Emma. Haven't you waited long enough? Then, if he doesn't feel the same, you have shared your heart and can move on with no regrets. You know I am right."

They continued to talk, but she changed the subject. As the lunch ended, he was planning his night with Jane.

He told Emma one more thing before they left. "If

you walk away, then you walk away, but don't walk away from him again without a goodbye. You have to have closure. If you don't get out of the past, you will never find your now. Emma, go find your now before it's too late. Go back and *at least* get your heart. You owe that much to yourself."

It was time for Alec to go, and she hugged him goodbye promising to think about what he said.

EMMA WALKED INTO the shop where her mom was busy working on flowers for a wedding. "Hey sweetie," Ella said steadily working on the bridal bouquet.

"Hey, Mom. I am going upstairs. Need anything?"

"Hey, I saw Darby at the post office earlier, and she sent this box for me to take over to Mazi's for Drew — something sent from Julie with store supplies or something. Anyway, Mazi said he's moving out to the cabin today. So would you take it to him for me?"

She was stunned because that was the first she'd heard about him moving, but she tried to hide the surprise from her mother. "Sure. Where is it?"

"Right behind you," she said never looking up.

"Okay. I'll get it to him. Actually, I'm about to go meet with some contractors and need to talk to him first anyway."

"Okay. I will see you later. Oh, and before I forget, keep up with the weather because I heard there was a strong line of storms headed this way."

"Sure. Will do, Mom."

With a quick, 'see ya later,' she picked up the box

and was on her way to attempt to do the hardest thing she could imagine—face the truth—talk to Drew, but mostly tell him goodbye. Today was the day her life would change forever.

EMMA WALKED INTO the mansion and looked around one last time. She knew it had been a mistake to come back. As she walked through the place she loved, tears began threatening her eyes again. She climbed the new staircase and briefly stepped out on the balcony that overlooked much of the town.

A few minutes later it was time to leave. Gazing upon the place once more, she closed the door behind her and wiped her tear-filled eyes. Saying goodbye to the love of her life was harder than she thought it would be. She could not imagine how much harder it was going to get when she finally faced Drew. If she could only have one more time to see herself deep inside his eyes — to feel him hold her close enough that she could hear his heart beating. The longing she felt was overwhelming. If he could just be hers one more time — one more day. She'd already memorized his face, his touch, his embrace, and he would always remain in the deepest part of her. That was better than not having him at all.

Chapter Sixteen

*"Once in a while, right in the middle of an ordinary life,
Love gives us a fairytale.
~Author Unknown*

Emma drove her Jeep down to the cabin, and from the distance, she saw him carrying a box into his new home. By the time she stopped, she had to take several deep breaths and keep reminding herself to breathe. She kept saying to herself, "You can do this. Just breathe. Put one foot in front of the other."

This was the last thing she wanted to do, but she knew it was something she had to do in order to have any sort of life. This was the only way. It was time to let Drew go. It was time to say goodbye. Of all the times she had rehearsed her goodbye she never expected him looking quite so good. Why was he in his faded jeans with his shirt unbuttoned? It was almost more than she could take seeing his toned abs. Then suddenly, he spotted her.

Drew stopped when he saw her walking toward him. She had not contacted him in weeks, directly anyway, and she had made it perfectly clear she had no interest in ever doing so. And now, here she was, standing just in front of him.

She carried the box from her Jeep and walked toward him thinking she'd drop it at any moment. It was heavy, and she was relieved when he lifted it from her arms.

"Hey, Emma. What is this stuff?"

"Darby sent this to you. Julie sent it by accident or something — said it belongs to you. I see you are moving?"

"Yeah, seemed like the right time." In a distance, the thunder began to roll, and the storm clouds seemed to be moving in. Looking up at the sky, he said, "Looks like we may get some rain."

"Yeah. It does." She stood in the awkward silence, searching for words.

"Would you like a drink? Sorry, fresh out of unsweetened tea, but how about a bottle of water? Or, I have a beer."

"I'll take a beer." She thought a little liquid courage might be just what she needed.

They stepped inside the cabin, and he went to the refrigerator to get her a beer.

"So, how's the house coming along? Any new developments I need to know about?" he asked opening the bottle and handing it to her.

After taking a few large sips, she finally said, "About that. Drew, I really need to tell you something."

"Okay. Shoot."

She could not take it anymore. She sat down on the couch, aware that he could see the emotion all over her.

"Emma, is something wrong? Are you okay?" he asked as he walked over and placed his hand on her shoulder.

She pushed him away and moved so he wouldn't be touching her, and finally, she found her words and blurted them out. "I can't do this anymore, Drew.

This project — this house, us, or what we used to be anyway."

Totally not expecting this, he responded with, "What? I don't…"

"Drew, I just cannot do this — pretend to be your friend. All of it — it's too much. It's not fair to me — to you,"

"What is going on? I don't …"

"This — pretending nothing ever happened between us."

"Emma, you told me not to talk about it. You haven't even spoken to me for weeks."

"What about seven years ago, Drew? Where were you then? Why didn't you have the guts to tell me to my face that you didn't love me anymore? Instead, you sent your sister — your sister that *hates* me, by the way," she said strongly through her tears she no longer tried to hold back. "Why, Drew? Tell me! I want to understand!" she shouted.

"Me? *Me?*" He stood up, ran his fingers through his hair, and then hit the wall, raising his voice. "First of all, if I remember correctly, *you* were the one that came back from you trip with a change of heart and with Alec! *You* were too much of a coward to tell me yourself! *You* had my sister tell *me!*" He stopped ranting and took a few deep breaths to calm himself then turned and in a much softer tone asked her, "Was I that easy to replace, Em? Oh, excuse me. *Emma*."

Emma could hardly believe the words coming from his mouth. What did he just say? What was he talking about? Her head was spinning and for a minute she thought she would faint at what she was afraid she was hearing. He was still speaking and she was trying to understand. How she desperately wanted, no needed, to understand.

"I was so ready to see you," he started to say but had to stop because tears threatened to choke his words. With tears mixed with hurt and anger, he continued as she listened. He stared out the window as he spoke. "Emma, I counted down every second of that day. Hell, I counted down the entire summer until you were back, but that day finally arrived, and my Em was coming home. God, I missed you like crazy.

"That day, I lost my phone so I couldn't text or call you when I realized my 'quick' trip to the building supply for Julie was going to be much longer than I had anticipated. By the time I finally arrived, you were gone. I never saw you again." He turned around, and she saw fresh tears as he wiped them from his eyes. "Was I not even worth a goodbye?"

By now, rain was falling outside as fast as Emma's tears. The information was unbelievable, and she tried to piece together what she thought he was saying to her. She began to cry harder now "Drew, I didn't. She told me…" She stopped to catch her breath.

"Who? What are you talking about?" he snapped.

"Julie. Julie told me you didn't love me anymore — that you had fallen out of love with me," she said almost frantically.

"No way," he said defensively. "She would never do that to me, Emma. How could you make up such a thing? I know you two don't get along but…"

"Drew, I swear to you!" She realized he'd believe Julie over her, and then she said with defiance, "Know what? It doesn't even matter — not anymore! I'm out of here. Have a nice life. I won't *ever* bother you again."

THE *Point*

She ran out, slamming the door behind her.

"Emma wait!" he shouted over the approaching storm. He began to pick up speed to reach her before she could get away. Finally, he reached out and grabbed her arm. "This storm looks really bad and the wind is…"

"I will not stay here and listen to you call me a liar, Drew. I came here to tell you that I am done. I am leaving, and you don't have to worry about me ever again. You and Julie can live happily ever after for all I care, but I have spent my last day worrying about you. I hope you two will be very happy," she said with fire in her eyes. She then jerked her arm from his grasp and ran toward her Jeep.

Right on her heels, he chased her until he grabbed her with his entire body. Shouting over the rain, he said, "You can't leave — not like this!"

"I can and I am! Let go of me, Drew!"

"No!" Then he said with the realization that was at hand in a much softer tone. "I won't let you go again. I'll never let you go again." Then before he knew it, be said out loud, "I love you too much."

"What?" she asked in staggering disbelief. It was as if time were standing still and there was no storm raging around them. It was just the two of them.

"I love you, dammit. I do." He softened his tone to a whisper realizing what he'd said and repeated the words again. "I love you, Em."

As the rain poured all around them, he pulled her toward him, and with seven years of unacknowledged passion and feelings pent up inside him, he kissed her before she could say another word. Then he picked her up, threw her over his shoulder, and carried her back inside the cabin while she kicked and screamed.

He brought her some towels and one of his shirts because she was soaked. They both were. He sat down beside her, stared at her, and said, "We are about to have a long, overdue talk — right here, right now — whether you want to or not."

"Drew it's not…"

"Hey, it's non-negotiable, Emma. For once in your life, calm your fiery, hot head down and listen." She opened her mouth to speak, and he said a quick, "Shh." Finally, he began to speak, "Well, first of all, now you know. I finally said it. I love you." Then, in a much softer tone, he said, "Emma, I never stopped loving you. I was going to come find you so many times, but I couldn't come. I just couldn't get past the letter."

"So she at least gave you my letters?"

"What letters? I got part of one she said you dropped and a t-shirt you sent, and — oh yeah, a picture of you and Alec on some beach in Greece. Hey, at least it was the part with your confession on it, so I wasn't left totally in the dark."

"Drew. What are you talking about? What confession? That I loved you? The only letters I gave her were a few letters I had written you. I knew I couldn't mail them on time for you to respond back, so I just decided to hand them to you in person. I wrote because we couldn't call each other — not really, and I had to talk to you, so I wrote letters. I missed you so much I thought I'd die. You weren't the only one with the countdown going on."

"Julie handed me a letter that YOU wrote saying that you were too young to know what real love is. Sound familiar?" he said coldly.

"I never—" she began, but he bitterly interrupted and continued.

"How you were being held back and you needed to see the world," he said with increasing volume. "There was more, but I think you know exactly what I am talking about."

His face was stern and his tone was just as sharp as the look on his face.

"Drew, while I did write that, I believe Julie only gave you part of that letter. I was explaining how someone said that to me and I didn't believe it. I never did anything but miss you. The longer I was away, the more I knew…" She hesitated but finally said, " I knew you were the only one I loved and ever would love."

Her words stunned him. A look of relief mixed with realization washed over his expression at once.

"But Emma, why would Julie do that? No. There's got to be an explanation. I almost died right before her that summer. I barely made it out alive. You were my heart. I hurt so bad I could barely breathe." He said in astonishment. By his expression, Emma realized some huge misunderstanding had taken place.

They talked, and as the time passed, the storm continued to intensify. Before they knew it, the electricity was knocked out with a large clap of thunder following. It was already dark out, so instinctively they reached for one another.

"Let's find some candles." He spoke softly.

Even though he could not see her eyes, he felt them. He could feel them being drawn to one another, deep inside. There, in the darkness, he placed his hand on her face and drew her to him once again. Only this time, he very tenderly kissed her before letting go of her to get a candle. Not a word was spoken, but in the stillness, they both knew what they once had shared was still there. Their love. He walked away and found several candles. When he lit them, he could actually see her face again.

They sat in the middle of the floor, still in shock. They were slowly beginning to realize everything they believed had been a lie. In the soft candlelight, he once again placed his hands on her face. He gently kissed her lips then held her face in his hands, and with his thumb, he traced the frame of her face.

He spoke softly to her. "Emma, do you have any idea how much I have missed you? Every day of my life, I have missed you. I waited for so long. I thought I would give you time so I could someday give it all back to you, but after so much time passed, I never thought I would ever get this again — time with you." Then, brushing her hair off her face, he kissed her with all the passion he had.

"Drew," she said now holding his face in her hand. "I love you, Drew. I never stopped." Overwhelmed by emotion, she continued. "I tried to move on... many times, but you were always there, standing in front of me. I couldn't," she whispered as a tear rolled down her cheek. "We wasted so much time..."

He put his fingers on her lips, traced them, looked deep inside her eyes, and said, "I think it's time we get it all back, starting right now." She started to say something, but he brushed her lips with his fingertips. "Shh." He kissed her tear and then her lips. "Em, we are not missing any more... ever."

Then he told her to wait for a minute. He lit another candle and placed it in the bedroom. Then he came back, cradled her up into his arms, carried her, and placed her on his bed as he kissed her forehead. She had only taken her socks and shoes off in the other room before the lights went out, but her jeans were still damp. He was glad she hadn't taken them off because he wanted to do it. He wanted this moment to be one they would never forget. They had nowhere to go, with a storm raging outside, and loads of time to make up for.

There in the candle-lit room as she lay on the bed, he took her small foot into his hand and kissed the top of it never taking his eyes off hers. Then he ran his hand up her jeans and as he slowly unbuttoned the shirt he had given her moments before. The walls had come down and he no longer cared what emotions he allowed her to see in his eyes. Never taking his eyes off her, he slowly made his way down until each button was undone. As the shirt fell to the floor, he held her bare chest next to his and kissed her as he ran his hand down the small of her back. Then he lifted up from her and he kissed her stomach. Then, he began taking her jeans off. She, in turn, took his off, and then they made sweet, beautiful love like they had never experienced before.

Just lying there, he held her as if he were putting a piece of him back where it belonged. He asked, "Do you have any idea how perfect I feel right now?"

She laughed and said, "Well, maybe, since I feel the exact same way."

"Emma, I missed you so much. You know, at first, without you in my life, I thought I would die in the darkness. It was almost unbearable. I drank all the time — even almost got thrown out of college freshman year. I wanted to drink all the pain away, but it only got worse. Then, Darby came along…" he said as his voice began to trail off.

"Hey, it's okay. I'm with you now, and I'm here to stay," she said as she kissed his chest. He kissed the top of her head as she continued to speak. "I missed you, too. Did I ever. I used to try to imagine what this would be like… being in your arms again. It's better than I remembered or imagined."

"Baby, I could hold you in my arms like this forever. You fit just right."

"Then why don't you?" she said kissing the palm of his hand looking up at him.

Then, they made love again and again.

Neither of them wanted to leave the other's arms. This was their time and much time had been lost. As amazing as the night had been, they realized they had not eaten since lunch. Begrudgingly, they ventured out into the kitchen nook to look for food they could eat without having to cook since the electricity was still out. They found some crackers and grapes. They also managed to find a kerosene lantern that Drew had picked up from an antique store. Though he bought it for decoration, it actually worked. It gave off much more light than the candles. The rain steadily pounded outside, but the brunt of the wind and lightening had been long gone for some time. They couldn't care less and were both perfectly content to remain in this cabin and in each other's arms forever.

They spread out their picnic of crackers, grapes, and bottled water on the den floor. It was better than any five-star restaurant either of them had ever been to. In the shadows, Drew saw the box Emma brought over that Julie sent to Darby by accident.

"So, wonder what's in the box?" Drew asked as he walked over to put it beside them. "This should be good, Em. No telling what shameless, scandalous high school stuff is packed in here."

Emma propped up on him like he was the back of a chair and fed him grapes as she ate them as well. Because she was so small, he had no problem maneuvering the box with her right inside his arms. She was still processing all the events that had taken place. She had almost decided she was in some sort of wonderful dream. It was as if they had always been this way.

He kissed the top of her hair and started digging inside the box. The first thing he saw was his cell phone from years back — the one he "lost."

"Here's my phone," he said with little shock.

She sat up and started looking, too. "My pictures, I gave them to her to give to you along with..." she said as he pulled up the rest of the stash "my letters." Then, repulsed at the thought of what Julie had done, she got angry all over again. "She is such a... a... What in the hell did I ever do to make her hate me this bad?"

"Damn her." He swore underneath his breath. "Let me just say it's a good thing she's gone for a week because I don't think I could handle her right now."

"You're right. We need time to cool down," she agreed.

Then, although the light was dim, she could still make out his facial expression as it turned from tension to what appeared to be sadness. "What is it now? What?"

She could make out tears on his cheeks as he handed her the letter and placed his hands over his face wiping them away quickly, but try as he might, the words he had just read touched his heart more than anything had all night — well almost anything.

"I told you she gave me a part of a letter. She said you dropped it. I think I just found the other half."

Emma picked it up and began to read it aloud.

> *Page 1*
> *August 5, 2004*
> *Dear Drew,*
>
> *I miss you terribly. I can hardly breathe from missing you so much. If I could just hear your voice, it may not hurt so much, but unfortunately, I can't so, I suffer.*
>
> *I'm so confused about school in the fall. I know my mom struggles being a single mom, and if I take this scholarship at the University of Alabama, it would be a load lifted from her. She has sacrificed so much for me over the years. Although she's never mentioned the tuition, I know it has to be an issue. But the thought of being apart from you again tears my soul in half. I can't endure this pain again, not like this. I am not good without you, Drew. If you ever wondered how deep my love for you is, let me just say this. I love you without ending.*
>
> *Page 2*
>
> *There is a lady from Birmingham that is chaperoning this trip. Her nephew, Alec Gresham, is also on this trip. She has really been pressuring me to take the internship opportunity because he is in the program too. He is a fun guy and the only*

friend I have made on this trip. Trust me; he has heard all about you and feels like you are old friends. I think you would like him, Drew. Anyway, his nosey aunt heard me talking to him about us the other day, and of course, she had smart comments to make. Before I knew it, she had me over to the side giving me her take on what she thought about me and my outlook on life.

Page 4

I heard her, but it only confirmed what I already knew. I love you. I love who I am when I'm with you. You are my heart, Drew Dalton, and we have the real thing. What we are and what we share together is magic. For now, I can only dream of where you are, but I am counting the seconds when I have you in my arms, and when that time comes, I am never letting you go again, EVER.

See you soon.

I love you. I love you. I completely and totally love you,

With all I am,

Em

"So, I am guessing she *only* gave you page three since that page is missing. Drew, she planned all of this. She watched both of us spiral into a deep, dark place that we almost didn't return from. Who does something like this? And why?"

"Em," he said as he held her close to him and felt her heart beat into his. "Em, how did we ever believe, or not know, that we were meant to be? How did we fall for this?"

"Drew, we were so young, and it was your sister. There is no way we could've known. We can't blame ourselves. Let's just be thankful we are here now… that we found each other again. Let's live in the now. I am tired of the past."

"Emma, you're right." Then he kissed her again holding her face. "Tonight is the beginning of our always." He kissed her again.

Then he blew the candles out, carried the love of his life again to the bedroom, and held her in his arms promising to never let go.

Chapter Seventeen

"Sometimes you wake up from a dream-sometimes you wake up in a dream. And sometimes, every once in a while, you wake up in someone else's dream."
~Richelle Mead

The morning sun filled the cabin bedroom window. At first, Emma thought it had all really been a dream, but within seconds, she saw Drew coming toward her with a single flower in his hand. She knew it wasn't a dream but more like a dream come true.

"Good morning, my beautiful lady." He kissed her softly. He handed her the daisy explaining that was the best he could do because her yellow flowers weren't in bloom.

"This is perfect." She kissed him, and she got out of the bed placing the flower behind her ear. "You are perfect. *We* are perfect."

"Come with me because I have a surprise for you." He held out his hands for hers.

Stepping outside, he led her to the pier where he had a picnic breakfast prepared.

"How did you *do* all this? *When* did you do all this?"

"I still have my ways." He laughed as they sat down to blueberry muffins and freshly squeezed OJ, complements of Mazi's. "Just because we have been apart doesn't mean I had amnesia. I remember well that you sleep like a rock, so I left while you were sound asleep. I wanted to surprise you when you woke up. I felt like you worked up quite an appetite last night." She playfully hit him and smiled. "And for dessert, tah- dah." He lifted the napkin. It was an apple and a jar of peanut butter.

"Aww, you remembered. But I didn't know you got dessert with breakfast."

"I told you, I remember everything." He kissed her on the nose. "And today, anything is possible. It really rained a lot last night. The wind must have been strong too because limbs and even a few trees were down over by the Millers' place, but it sure is beautiful today."

Looking at him she said, "Yes, it is beautiful, and I thought it was actually beautiful last night."

"So what do you want to do today, Em? You don't mind if I call you that do you, Em?"

She spoke through her smile and said, "I am pretty sure I heard you say it a few times last night."

"Oh, I hope you don't mind, but I stopped by and let your mom know where you were so she wouldn't worry more than I knew she already had been since you didn't come home last night. She said she felt like you and I were together. I swear that woman has psychic abilities sometimes."

"That's my mom. Hey, your mom is just as bad. If I didn't know better, I'd thought she set all this up, down to the timing of the storm." She laughed.

"I didn't even tell Mom yet. We can both go tell her later in person." He winked. "I promised Benji yesterday I would take him fishing later today. If I had only known we were about to happen I would have…"

"You would have done the same thing. This is our life, and it starts today. Let's live in the now and live every second. Let's never take us for granted again."

"That's a deal," he agreed giving her a quick kiss. Then they finished up breakfast.

"Hey, Em, remember last night when we talked about how we were going to make up for all the lost time? Let's start right now. What are we going to do first? Anything you want."

She looked at him and smiled.

They ran to the falls where they were heading the day Julie interrupted them. It had been years since they had been out there, and it was as beautiful as they remembered.

"Em, look." He pointed at the old rope swing Daddy D fixed for them when they were in junior high. "Come on."

They played like they were twelve years old again. They took turns swinging the rope over the creek bank as it took them over the water and to the base of the falls then dropping into the freezing water that rushed down from the mountain. They swam finally stopping to rest on a rock behind the falls, which had seemed like a mysterious cave when they were younger.

As children, they played pirates most of the time there unless Emma could talk Drew into playing mermaids. They swam there as teenagers too, but today it all seemed different somehow. Although it looked the same, they were certainly different. It was like they were on a deserted island where no one existed except them.

He had been looking at her for some time when she finally asked, "What?" She started feeling her hair and face asking, "Is something on me?"

Without hesitation he simply kissed her without

even closing his eyes and then said as he brushed his hand over her wet hair, "Your hair, your face — you. It's all just right. Emma, do you have any idea how much I love you? I can't…"

His eyes continued to penetrate through her as he continued searching for words. He scooted up to a larger rock and leaned back on it as she leaned back on him, snuggled just under his chin with his arms wrapped around her to keep her warm. He held her close and said, "It's just, I never thought I'd have this back again. I never thought I would feel the way you only can make me feel… so alive. You give my life meaning, Em."

She leaned over and kissed his arm, and he leaned down and kissed the nape of her neck. "I had dreams about this, about us. The only times I truly felt alive over the past years is when I would find you in my dreams. I know that sounds crazy. It even sounds crazy to me when I hear myself say it aloud. It felt awful being engaged knowing I was still in love with you, but I had just accepted it as a part of who I was… a part I'd carry with me always."

They sat in silence for a little while longer, and then Emma confessed, "Drew, I used to dream about you, too." She stroked his hand with her thumb as she spoke. "I felt like if I could find you in my dreams and somehow you would know it… in your soul. Maybe in some twisted way, you did. Now who sounds insane?"

"Well, baby, we are a little insane, but I love it." They laughed and gave each other a quick kiss, and he said, "But at least we can be insane together." Then he picked her up, and under the falls they went. They raced to the edge and got out to dry off.

Back at the cabin, they took the top off the Jeep. "Hop in. I am driving," Emma said.

"Em, how are you coming on your driving skills these days?" he said shakily.

"I'm as good of a driver as always. Hang on."

Buckling up, he confessed, "That's what I was afraid of." He laughed and kissed her cheek.

Pulling up to the mansion, they couldn't believe all the water. In reality they knew it was only a shallow puddle in the yard but it gave the appearance of a small lake. They got out and noticed one of the carpenters in the yard picking up trash and walked over to speak to him.

"Well, it did rain last night," Emma remarked to the man, slightly laughing. "I didn't notice," she said while smugly smiling at Drew.

The construction worker didn't catch on to her inside joke, but Drew did.

The worker replied back, "Yes ma'am it was quite a storm last night. I am surprised you didn't hear it." She laughed, looked at Drew blushing at the thought of the night they'd just had. She agreed and the man continued to talk. "Drew, I am afraid this is what's left of the yellow tape that environmentalist group spent so much time putting into place last week." He said holding his hands out for Drew to see. He continued, "It is all gone, but the storm did not blow the little flag away. I left it so it can easily be found by the group so they won't have to comb the area searching again. It shouldn't be a problem. Seems like a waste of time to me anyhow. No one has even noticed that well in all these years, and chances are, they aren't ever going to."

"It's a tiny little flag. I don't think it would do much

in the way of alerting anyone if they didn't know it was there, " he said frowning at the sad, threadbare marker. "But you are probably right, no one ever had a problem before. Still, make a note to get something more visible to mark this with and make it weather proof."

The man made a note on his clipboard and continued the survey.

As Emma stopped to take a good, deep breath of reality, she realized how close she had come to walking away again. Away from Drew, the house, everything. She looked over at Drew and said, "I really was going to quit yesterday. I was so close. I don't know if I would've ever come back again either."

He came to her side, kissed the top of her head, and said, "The past is over. Today, this is where we are, and we are going to make it count — forever." She looked up and smiled at him. Then, he said with a grin, "I'm sure glad you changed your mind because good help is hard to find."

She hit him on the shoulder, and they started wrestling right there in the muddy, wet yard. Before they knew it, it was a contest to see who could get the most mud on the other one. Catching their breaths, they finally called a truce

"It's good to be back, Mr. Dalton."

"It's good to have you back, Miss Ashby."

"Emma, we're filthy," he laughed a real laugh. "I still have to go check on something in the house. Maybe they'll meet me at the back door."

She had never been more content in her life as they walked back to the old place.

They finally left and went back to the cabin to shower, and then they decided it was time to give the

Leyton townspeople something to talk about besides the angry little preacher at the church on the corner. So this time, Drew drove her Jeep. He told her he thought that would add to the buzz in town, but the truth was that she was an awful driver.

So, on a Saturday afternoon, while the lunchtime crowd gathered, Drew Dalton and Emma Ashby entered The Mazi Daze Café, arm in arm. They laughed and laughed. They couldn't help smiling even if they tried not to. Every single eye was on them, and what made it even better was when they sat down, they saw Jane and Alec at the table next to them. Then they laughed some more.

"Hey you two. Looks like somebody has something to tell her friend. Get over here you guys," Jane insisted while smiling with a wink.

From the looks on Jane and Alec's faces, they seemed to have enjoyed the stormy night too.

"So, Emma, when are you going to be wrapping up here and coming back to Alabama?" Alec asked.

That hit her like a ton of bricks. She had not thought one time in the past twenty-four hours about how this new relationship would affect her future. Now was not the time to hash through it though. It could wait.

"I am not sure," she said remembering about living in the moment then added, "But, it's not today."

"Well, I am heading back first thing in the morning. I will tell them you are still among the living. They'll never believe me when I tell them you were laughing and smiling *and* having fun."

"Ha. You make me sound so dull," she sarcastically joked.

"Well, you truly look like a different person. Love

looks good on you, Emma."

"Well, Alec, it feels pretty good on me, too." She shrugged up against Drew's arm. "And, if I may say so, it looks pretty good on both of you, as well."

"Why thank you," Jane said as Alec kissed her hand.

"Hey, what about me?" Drew asked smiling.

"Oh, it looks the very best on you, baby." Emma puckered her lips at him and winked.

The friends ate lunch, and then Emma and Drew walked next door to see her mom who was delighted to see her daughter in such a euphoric state. They visited a little while before continuing their rounds out to his parents. They could hardly wait to tell them the news.

When they pulled up and got out of the Jeep, they saw Daddy D and Benji outside filling the bird feeders.

"Uncle Drew!" Benji said with a squeal, running and jumping into his arms.

"Emmy Em." Andrew Dalton was as thrilled to see her.

"Hey Daddy D." She ran to hug him but refrained from jumping in his arms.

"Where's Mom?" Drew asked.

"Mrs. Liza, we have company," Daddy D called out in his sneaky, 'I've got a secret' voice.

Liza stepped outside onto the front porch and looked at them knowingly. "Emma, Drew. Emma *and* Drew," she said, beside herself.

"Uncle Drew. Look what I can do." Benji spit as far as he could.

"Emma, let's go inside," Liza said. "They are disgusting."

The ladies laughed and walked inside the house.

Mrs. Liza walked back to the counter where she had been in the process of sealing her homemade apple butter into glass mason jars. Emma sat on the kitchen stool, drinking a glass of water. She noticed baskets with apples strewn all around the place. Before she could even ask what she was going to do with all the apples, Liza was back to her task.

"Emma, it's so good to see you two together, where you both belong. He has been like a lost little boy without you all these years."

"I felt the same way... lost," she said placing her glass onto the counter.

"Well, I am thrilled. We missed you... all of us."

"Well, not all of you, Mrs. Liza."

"Oh, Julie... Emma," she started.

"No," Emma interrupted. "I don't won't to talk about it, not today. This is our new day, and it is a celebration."

"Okay, but..."

"Another day, okay? I am just so happy," she said and picked up an apple.

The ladies changed the subject and enjoyed the moment at hand. "So, tell me about the house," Liza said.

An excited Emma spent the next half hour talking about the plans they had made and caught her up on the progress already taking place. Emma told her all about the house. She could feel herself lighting up inside and wondered if it showed on her own face the same way it did on Drew when he started talking about the house.

Liza was finishing up her canning about the time Emma was finished describing their latest vision for the old place. They then went back outside to look for the guys and found them getting fishing gear together.

Drew came over to her and said, "Hey, Em, I am going to catch a ride with Dad and Benji back to the cabin. They are coming over to fish. Meet you there?"

"I'll tell you what. I am headed to the grocery store to get some food for your bare cupboards, okay?" she asked walking toward the Jeep. "I'll see you there soon. Need anything besides crackers and grapes?" she asked with a wink. He laughed a cute laugh, and she asked, "Seriously, want me to bring you back anything in particular?"

"Just you. You are all I want," he said giving her a quick kiss through the window.

"Okay, you dork, that is a given. I am afraid you are stuck with me." She kissed him back. "Ask your parents if they would like to come for dinner tonight," she said while driving away. "Oh and Drew, I love you," she yelled out her window as she pulled away.

Then he yelled back, "I love you more — and ask your mom to come, too."

THE FAMILIES GATHERED on that July evening as they had hundreds of times before, but tonight, there was a peace amongst them knowing two lost souls had finally found their way home. Everyone had an extra dose of contentment and happiness. Although this day had been perfect, the underlying fact that it would soon all come to an end escaped no one's mind. However, as Emma and Drew had clearly stated to them all, this day was to celebrate their love — period. No talking about Julie… not yet.

After a day of playing, fishing, grilling with the family, and playing endlessly with Benji, Emma and Drew were exhausted.

"It's been a good day, Drew."

"It's been the perfect day, Em."

"It's getting late. I had better be going."

"No, stay. Don't go."

"Drew, you know that we are already giving the good reverend a run for his money when it comes to be the talk of the town. I would hate to knock the little fellow out of his top earned position. Besides, you'll get sick of me."

He gave her a serious look and said, "Don't you know that I want you with me, always? I am more me with you than I ever am without you. We are stronger in every way, together."

"I agree, but I am not going to shack up with you down here, mister. It's just *not* going to happen." She kissed him a few more times, almost getting sucked back into staying, but was finally able to pry herself away. "I will see you tomorrow, you. Goodnight."

"Goodnight, Em. I love you so much," he said kissing her once more and putting her in her Jeep.

Finally, she drove back to the shop. On the drive, Emma thought about leaving. She knew that going back to Alabama was going to be almost impossible.

Chapter Eighteen

"Love doesn't make the world go round,
love is what makes the ride worthwhile."
~Elizabeth Barrett Browning

Time seems to fly when all your dreams come true. Before they knew it, the week was almost over. They still had one more Julie-free day, and they planned on enjoying every second of it.

First, they had to meet with the construction crew to finalize the details on the renovations. All the decisions seemed easier now that they had joined forces. There was one problem, however. Emma had struggled with adequate spacing for some of the productions they envisioned having there. That was what the meeting was for today. There was nowhere to set up a band or proper sound equipment and certainly no place for a sound room on the premises.

Emma and Drew proposed to go beyond the old barn and clear all the land between the grove and the mansion to build an outdoor amphitheater. This would allow them to attract local and possibly national talent. This would also afford them the space to create a sufficient equipment room to operate the sound and light, without compromising space *or* taking away from the feel of the house.

Emma could use her advertising background to promote theater productions and draw attention to the entire town of Leyton. This would be especially beneficial during the summer when vacationers were camping at the nearby National Park. There were so many possibilities for the project, and all of them would benefit the entire community. Drew and Emma also wanted to turn a portion of the house into an art gallery to would highlight local talent, the way her father had once dreamed of doing.

"Sounds good — sounds really good," the contractor said. "We'll have our architect draw up some plans and have you take a look Monday."

"Great," Drew said. They shook hands and said goodbye.

Drew and Emma's next stop was the building supply. They had a little painting project to do at the cabin, and then Drew had a special surprise planned for her later that night. It was the last night they'd share before the Julie storm blew back into town.

Emma cranked up her music. He smiled when a Springsteen came on, and said, "My baby's got 80's. See, not so bad is it?" She laughed and agreed. "Hey, do you remember when you were little you thought Bohemian Rhapsody was about algebra?" He laughed as he poked her side.

"You don't know what you're even talking about, you nut," Emma replied.

"Oh I remember well. I can still hear you singing at the top of your lungs. 'The algebra has a devil for the side of me... for me, for me...'" They both laughed.

They made it to the building supply and back to the cabin to paint quickly. This was more of a 'touch up' paint job than a full-blown painting job, but if it required a paintbrush, then to Emma, it was a real paint job. So, they got into old clothes and began to paint away. They painted one another from time to time. They made up dances, rewrote song lyrics, and made the most of the time they had.

"Hey, Em," he called her name, and as she turned around the paintbrush swept across her face.

"Really? You are going there?" She brushed the paint across his face.

He swiped her once again painting a stripe down her shirt saying, "I know—right." Then it was on.

They chased each other, and finally she dropped the brush screaming and laughing when he caught her out in the field—in the middle of the flowers. He scooped her up and tackled her to the ground rolling her all around. He decorated her hair with flowers. They kissed and then were up playing chase again.

She made her way to the porch to get a water bottle, and while drinking it she turned it toward him and squirted him before running. She ran in circles until he caught her, and this time he put her over his shoulder, carried her to the lake, and threw her in. Then, of course, he jumped in after her and they played some more.

The day had been the perfect ending to the dream they had lived for the entire week. Emma wished time could just stop. No jobs — no Julie. How amazing would that be? She knew the time was passing, and even though she tried not to let that enter into her thoughts, it was always lingering in the background threatening to rob her.

"Okay, Miss Ashby, I have a special night planned

for us, so I need you to do me a favor, okay?"

"What?"

He stopped, walked over, and looked at her all wet with specks of paint and one flower still stuck in her hair. He smiled and kissed her on the nose. "You are so damn adorable. Every time you look at me, you touch my heart. Do you have any idea how incredibly in love with you I am, woman?"

"Hope so," she teased.

"Well, you have my heart, body, and soul. I love you, so much," he said with a kiss on one cheek, then another, "I love you," followed by another kiss on the opposite cheek, then a third and final, "I love you, Emma," followed by a passionate kiss on her lips. "Okay. I have got to walk away right now or we aren't going anywhere but inside." He took a step back, holding his hands high in the air. "Go, go now," he said still reeling himself in from the sudden stir of passion. "Go to the shop, get dressed up, and I will pick you up around seven-ish, your time — real time, about 7:30 p.m." He looked into her eyes and kissed both of her hands never breaking his stare. "Is it a date?"

"It's three o'clock now — I think I can make it. You, sir, have yourself a date."

"Okay, I'll pick you up about 7:30."

"Alright, I'll see you around 7:30-ish…"

With a short, sweet kiss, he playfully kicked her on her rear end.

WHEN HE FELT he had given her ample time to be off

the property, he headed to the mansion to see if all his plans were underway. As planned, Mama El and Mrs. Liza were on flower detail — white roses were everywhere. However she managed it, he didn't know, but the flower of the night was there right in front of him — a yellow daffodil. He only needed one, but thankfully, they came planted in a pot so he got to choose his favorite.

Jane and Alec were in charge of getting the table and chairs. Jane had also volunteered to get the white linen tablecloth, the china, crystal stemware, and as many white candles as she could find. She was more than happy to be a part of this. She and Alec both were.

Darby and Moose were even involved in the scheme. They were to keep Emma distracted during her spare time. Moose said he was helping Mazi with a leaky water valve and would come take a few breaks at the shop. She had no idea he was just lurking around to make sure she didn't just decide to go anywhere. To make sure she didn't venture next door to investigate, Darby just happened to stop by to say hello and brought her a tea. Emma may have gotten suspicious had she not been so preoccupied about what she was going to wear for her date with Drew. She was grateful for Darby's input.

"Darby, is this weird? I mean, people aren't friends with each other when they have history like we do, are they?"

"Well, I don't know, but for once everything seems right — to me anyway. I am happy. Calvin makes me happy. Really happy."

"I am so glad for both of you, and I am glad you are my friend, Darby. Thanks for everything. And Drew does have good taste in women, I must say." Emma gave her a smirk.

"Emma, I really hope you know how much he really loves you. He is a totally different person with you. You glow all over him."

Emma just shrugged her shoulders and smiled a mischievous smile that said 'I know.'

So, with Darby and Moose keeping a close eye on Emma for the rest of the afternoon, Mama El worked her flower magic. Jane and Alec worked on everything else down to the roomful of white candles and the chilling champagne. Drew had one more task at hand — the most important one of all. He left to see his mom.

"Mom? Hey, Mom. Where are you?" Drew called walking through the back door.

"In my bedroom, Drew. Come on back."

"Hey, Mom. Got something for me?" he said with overwhelming pride.

"Drew, come sit down. I want to tell you something — something I should have told you a long time ago."

"Okay. You sound serious."

"It is serious. I am just sorry that today is the day you have to hear this."

"Mom, there is not anything you can say that can affect me today — nothing."

"Drew, you know how much we love Emma. She has seemed like part our family since the day she was born."

"I know, Mom. So are you saying I have your

blessing?" he asked still half-jokingly.

"Drew, I am really needing you to hear me," she said in a tone that concerned him.

"Okay, Mom. I am listening." He put all joking aside and joined her on the bedside.

"This ring I have in my hand belonged to your great grandmother, Clara Hastings. She was a lovely lady. She was my grandmother, but after Julie was born, she was actually more of a mother to me. She and my grandfather had a rare, once-in-a-lifetime love that reminds me so much of the love you share with Emma. That is the main reason I never offered it to you earlier when you proposed to Darby. I knew she wasn't your true love, your soul mate. Do you know how it feels in my heart that you and Emma found your way back to each other after all these years?" She stopped to take a tissue from his hand that he held out for her.

Puzzled, he then asked, "So why are you so sad, Mom? Are you not happy for us?" He patted her on the back only to realize there was more.

"Drew, you have got to hear the rest of this story. I should have told you, like I said, long ago so you could understand Julie better, but I have no choice but to tell you now. I just want you informed because of the fallout when she hears of your engagement. I am afraid it will be, well, an ordeal, to say the least."

So Liza proceeded to spend the next hour telling the story, which left Drew in shock. He left the house wondering how he could continue with his plans for the night in light of this information. How could he shake the melancholy that now dominated his heart? Then he remembered something that Emma had said earlier — that they had to live in the now. She was right.

Tomorrow, they could put some missing pieces of the puzzle together, but tonight, he was proposing to the lady who held his heart. No matter what the condition, it belonged to her, and tonight, he was going to ask Emma Ashby to be his wife.

He arrived at her house promptly at 7:20 knowing he'd still have to wait at least twenty more minutes or so. That was perfect because Mazi was delivering the meal at 7:30. He could not believe how excited, nervous, and overwhelmed he was. He had no doubt he was doing the right thing, but he never anticipated being so nervous. He wore his black pants, white shirt, and black coat, without a tie.

It was a little late to think about it now, but they had never seriously talked about getting married. What if she wanted to go slow? What if she wasn't ready? His mind raced. Every insecurity he ever had was choosing this moment to come out. He knew he had to get a hold of himself or he'd be a wreck before the night even began. He took a few extremely deep breaths, and then Emma descended the staircase. The mere sight of her made all other concerns fade. Emma dressed in a black dress with her hair pulled up, and she was all that mattered in Drew's world.

"You look stunning." He spoke softly kissing her hand. Taking her arm, he escorted her to the car. She had a special glow about her tonight — more than usual, he thought.

Before they knew it, they were at The Point, where

it all began.

"We're here."

"How perfect, Drew."

"Okay, you have to close your eyes, Em. I'll help you."

"This feels like déjà vu."

"Trust me?"

"I do. You know that."

He helped her into the house and carefully led her into the room. Then, in a soft whisper, he said, "Okay. Open your eyes."

EMMA COULD HARDLY believe her eyes. White roses were everywhere. White candles illuminated the entire room. White draped over anything resembling construction. Immediately, tears formed in her eyes, and she threw her arms around him.

"Drew. It's perfect. It's like a dream."

"Good. That's what I was going for, a dream come true — our dream." He kissed her hand and then pulled her chair out for her. They sat down to dinner. First, he poured the champagne and proposed a toast. "To our love."

After the toast, Mazi's waitress from the café served them. They ate, drank, and talked. The young lady left a covered, silver dessert tray on the buffet table beside them then said goodbye so they could be alone for the rest of the evening.

"Drew, this is more than I ever dreamed this night would be."

"It's just the beginning. I have more surprises."

"Oh really? How can you possibly top this, my dear?"

At that moment, he walked across the room and picked up his guitar he'd brought from the cabin. "You asked me if I ever learned to play. I told you I did learn to play just one song, and I think you may have heard it before."

The second she heard the first few chords she instantly knew what it was. Her hands covered her mouth as she became overcome with emotion. Tears streamed down her cheeks as Drew played and sang "Love of My Life."

When he was done, he put his guitar down, and while still on his knees, he reached over and kissed her. There in the candlelight, he could barely contain his own emotion. Choking up, he let the tears fall. He reached over, lifted the silver dessert tray, and presented it to her — a single yellow daffodil — her special flower. He gently picked up the flower, and when he focused her attention on the center of the bloom, she was astounded. It took a moment to come to her senses, but when she realized what was happening, she simply asked a question.

"Drew? Is this?"

He nodded his head yes as he wiped his own tears back and tried to regain his composure so he could talk. "Emma, you are my love — the only love I've ever known. When I look in your eyes, I see the man I want to be. I see us. You are my heart — my breath. I can't go on living this life without you — forever — for the rest of our lives. Emma Elizabeth Ashby, would you do me the honor of becoming my wife and making me the happiest man in the universe?" Then, wiping his tears, he asked again. "Please marry me, Em?"

Speechless, with tears of joy, she shook her head and fell into his arms and said an excited, "Yes, yes, yes. Of course, I'll marry you, Drew."

Then, he took the ring, placed it on her finger, and kissed it. Then he picked her up, swung her around, and passionately kissed her.

"Drew, I have always loved you," she said with a soft kiss. "Loving you has always been the best part of me. You truly are my soul mate."

He placed both hands on each side of her face and kissed her again. Then he said, "Emma, remember tonight because it's the beginning of our always."

"The safest place in my world is here in your arms, Drew. I feel like I'm home, finally."

"You are, Em. You are home. We're home, baby. Nothing will ever separate us again, ever."

"But what about Julie?"

"We are not ruining the night by discussing her. It's about us, okay?" he ignored the small voice nudging him to tell her now.

"Let's promise that we will hold onto each other with all the strength we have. We have to always keep us alive. We can't let Julie or anyone ever change that—not this time."

"Don't you know our love is forever? We are forever. True love never dies," he said into her hair as he kissed it.

"Drew, I was born to love you. Did you know that?" she asked as he gently kissed her neck. They made their way to the floor where he slowly laid her back on the pile of leftover white sheets, kissing him over and over.

THE *Point*

He kissed her with great passion, and they made the most beautiful love right in the very spot that they had the first time. They both knew that their love would now and always be real. No one accepted and loved them the way they always had loved one another. Deep in their souls, no words were needed. They knew this love would last forever because it was, as they were — timeless.

Chapter Nineteen

*"For everything you have missed, you have gained something else,
And for everything you gain, you lose something else."
~Ralph Waldo Emerson*

Liza and Andrew were playing one more round of Candy Land with Benji. It was already an hour past his bedtime, but this was his last night there so they all agreed that it would be okay. Halfway through the game, they saw headlights coming up the drive.

"Who in the world could that be at this time of night?" Liza asked worriedly.

"I bet it's Uncle Drew coming to tell me I am gonna get to have an Auntie Em just like on The Wizard of Oz."

While laughing, Andrew stood up from the game table saying, "Son, I bet the last person you see tonight will be Uncle Drew." He went to the back door to check it out.

"Who is it, dear?" Liza asked at the time she heard Benji shout, "Mommy!"

Liza Dalton felt fear strike through her and silently prayed that Benji didn't mention anything about Drew and Emma.

"Hey, Mommy," he said and gave her a giant hug and kiss. Then, he excitedly asked, "Guess what, Mommy, guess what?"

"Hello to you, too," she said and gave him a big

kiss back. "There better be a good reason you are up at this hour." She poked his ribs asking, "What's the big news?"

"*I'm* getting an Auntie Em — just like Dorothy on the Wizard of Oz. Except mine is a lot prettier."

It was clear by the look on Julie's face she was in shock. She sat, turned to Benji, and said, "Benji, I think Daddy D needs to read you a bedtime book and put you to bed. I just wanted to come in tonight and take you back early in the morning. Daddy is home waiting on us *and* if you go on to sleep, you'll get your surprise we brought you first thing in the morning, okay?"

"Okay, Mommy. I love you." He kissed her goodnight.

"Goodnight, baby boy. I love you, too."

The rage came over Julie the instant her son was out of sight. She was so angry, she didn't speak for a few minutes, which deeply concerned Liza. "Well, well, well, and I thought *I* would be the one *surprising you* all with my early arrival, but boy was *I* wrong."

"Now, Julie…"

"Don't *now Julie* me! What in the hell is going on? Drew asked her to *marry* him?"

"Julie, your brother—"

"My brother is an idiot!" she raged. "What makes her *so damn* special?"

"Your brother is in love, Julie. Let it go. This is not the time."

Julie cut her off saying, "Oh, it's the perfect time, mother. I have kept my mouth shut for eighteen years, and this is the last day it stays shut. It is high time she hears what I have to say."

"Julie, this night is so special for your brother — not

just Emma. Honey, can't you see how much he loves her? How much he always has?"

"Everybody loves Emma. *Emma. Emma. Emma!*" she screamed. "Do you have any idea how sick I am of hearing her name?"

Suddenly, Julie became calm and spoke in an even tone as she grabbed her keys from the table. "You know, I think it's time for a little family reunion." She left the house.

Liza knew where she was going. Liza frantically tried to reach Drew on his cell, but it went straight to voice mail. Of course, he didn't have it on. Why would he? She tried Emma's phone too, but she got her voice mail as well. When Andrew came in the room, she filled him in on what happened. They decided that Ella needed to know. She needed to be prepared for the fallout.

Ella was devastated but thankful for the warning. She and Liza decided to go meet them at the mansion because Emma's world was about to turn upside down, and it would take every one of them to explain it to her.

Julie was furious and getting madder with each mile she drove. She knew she'd find him at The Point. They loved that decrepit old place, which made her despise it all the more. She finally pulled up, stormed out of the car, and headed toward the house.

Drew heard someone outside and was halfway to the door when she ambushed them.

"Julie, you need to…"

"No, Drew," Emma said then paused. "Let her stay. It's about time we all had a talk," Emma insisted.

"Listen to your fiancée, Drew. I think she's right. It's time we all had a talk—a *real* talk. I think that is just what we need. All of us."

"I don't think this is the time or place, Julie," he said sternly.

"That's just it, little brother. No one around here thinks, now do they? Actually, this *talk* should have taken place long ago, but of course, everyone wanted to make sure *poor little Emma* was okay. Bless her heart," Julie spewed in a condescending tone.

"Julie, I am begging you," he pleaded. She would have no mercy on her little brother tonight. Tonight it all ended. The perfect world they had created would shatter into fragments tonight. It was ending this night.

"No, Drew. I *want* to hear this, and I want to hear it right *now*," Emma continued to persist.

Drew blew the candles out for fear Julie would set the place on fire she was so out of it, and they all sat down at the table.

"First of all, I am sure you two have compared notes and finally figured out that I was the reason you weren't together," Julie said. "We got in late this afternoon and took things by the shop. That's when I realized the wrong box was sent to the Leyton store by accident. So…" She glanced at Drew. "I guess you found your cell phone — and the letter. I knew I should have destroyed that box long ago. I actually forgot all about them until we began shuffling things around getting ready for a second store."

Emma blurted out, "How could you do that, Julie? You kept us apart, and Drew almost married someone he didn't even love. You *knew* how in love we were. What kind of sick, twisted mind even thinks something like that up?"

"I would love to know that myself, Julie. How could you be so heartless? So hateful? And how could you pick *this* night to bring all this up — tonight of all nights?" Drew asked.

With a smug, arrogant look, Julie continued, "Emma, I see you have *our* great grandmother's wedding ring? Of course you do." She continued, "Well, have you ever seen mine?" She placed her hand out so Emma could get a look.

Drew held his breath because he knew whatever she was leading up to was about to break Emma's heart.

"Do you know who *this* ring belonged to?" Julie asked

Emma shook her head no just as Julie knew she would. "Well, you see, *this ring* belonged to my *other* grandmother." As soon as she paused for a breath, she cut her eyes, to Emma and said, "My grandmother on the *Ashby* side. My daddy's mother. *Our* grandmother, Emma—as in yours and mine. You see, *Emmy Em*… Carter Ashby is my daddy, too."

Emma's head was swirling. Nothing made sense. Drew came and knelt beside her.

Finally, Emma said, "What are you talking about, Julie?"

"You see, *Emma dear,* you are my half-sister."

Emma felt the air leaving her body, and for a minute, she thought she might truly faint. She grabbed her head with her hand. Then she caught herself and said, "That is a lie. Why would you say something so cruel? Why would you blatantly lie like that? What is *wrong* with you?" Emma hissed.

Drew tried to comfort her by rubbing her back, and then he said softly, "It's true, Emma. She *is* your sister."

"No, Drew, she's lying as usual. There is *no way*. She's a liar. She's *lying*," she said as she shuddered head to toe.

Emma felt as if she had been stabbed in the heart. She got up in a breathless state; she could barely think. "Drew, you knew this? And you didn't *tell* me?"

"Emma, I just found out today, when I picked up the ring. Baby listen…"

"No!" Emma screamed. "This is a lie! A big, fat, Julie-made-up lie!"

At that moment, Ella Ashby and Liza Dalton came in the house.

Emma was so relieved to see her mother. She ran into her arms as she cried desperate tears saying, "Mom, tell her it's not true. She's a liar." She was shaking uncontrollably now.

"Emma, sweetheart, we should have told you long ago."

Emma had to sit down. She sat on the floor taking deep breaths feeling completely betrayed by everyone she loved. Drew and Ella both tried to put their arms around her, but she pushed them away. She sat on the floor rocking back and forth having a full-blown panic attack.

"Emma," Ella began. "When your father and I met, we instantly fell in love. I loved him from the first time I laid my eyes on him. It only took a few weeks to know I wanted to spend my life with him. After we dated about a month, he told me about Liza. They met the summer before they started college on a senior trip. He never even knew about Julie until later."

Then Liza joined in. "Your daddy was a wonderful man, Emma, a bit of a free spirit — but someone that would never have walked away from responsibility. My father, however, was furious, and your father was forbidden to come near any of us ever again. Poor Carter, he never even knew why. My father threw me out of his house because he said I had disgraced the entire family, and he could no longer even stand the sight of me when I refused to abort or give the baby up for adoption.

"So I lived with my grandparents from that moment on and was never close to my parents again. It divided the entire family because I simply chose to keep my baby — Julie. My grandparents were supportive, but my parents never got over it. That's why my grandfather left me everything and left my own father nothing. To them, I *was* their daughter. My father had nothing more to do with them either.

"After your dad graduated college, he was doing freelance work around the area, and I ran into him. I felt I must tell him about Julie, and of course, he wanted to meet her. He adored her, but we simply didn't love each other. By this time, I had met and fallen in love with Andrew. We were engaged. Julie was already three years old, and we thought it'd be best if Andrew adopted her after the wedding. He loved her just as if she had been his very own. He still does." She stopped to wipe her eyes with a tissue.

Then Ella came back into the conversation. "I met your father when I was eighteen, Emma. One of the first things he told me was about Julie. So we visited Leyton hoping to get to see her, and we did. Oh, he loved Julie, but she knew no other daddy except for Andrew. The four of us sat down and discussed the possibility of us moving to Leyton so Carter could be around and watch her grow up... so, we did. We planned on telling her when she was older, and we were about to when..."

Then Julie forced her way back into the conversation, "But no one counted on his plane crashing and him dying when I turned eighteen, did they? See, that's how *I* found out. The day he died, I overheard our parents talking. But, you see, it was not about *me* anymore. *Noooooo.* Everything from that moment on was to protect you, Emma. If I heard it once, I heard one million times about how you were too young to understand and blah, blah, blah, blah. So, I left for college and rarely came home, but the older I got, the angrier I got. So, see Emma, now, *you* know."

The room fell silent.

Then, Julie started up again. "When I came back from college, my parents and my little brother were more in love with you than ever," she said directly to Emma with venom. "They probably thought I was jealous, but I was just angry. Your daddy, our daddy, adored you. He spent every single moment being crazy over you, and then my own dad, Andrew, started calling you that stupid name — his 'Emmy Em.' Dad, Mom, Drew — they all worshiped you — little Miss Perfect.

"My brother thought of you more of a sister, when you were younger that is, than he did me. Then I will be damned if he didn't fall in love with you the first chance he got. There was no way I could allow that! You had taken *everything* from me. Everything! There was no way you were getting one more thing — until now." She finally said, "So how do you feel *now*, sister?"

Emma stood up in shock. She put her hands over her ears and screamed, "Stop it! I don't want to hear anymore. Everyone just leave me alone!"

She ran out the door sobbing uncontrollably. Drew immediately ran after her calling her name, but he stopped and looked Julie in the eyes and said, "I will *never, ever* forgive you for what you've done tonight — *ever!*" He slammed the door and ran into the night desperately searching for Emma.

It didn't help matters any that another storm was blowing in. As the thunder rolled in the distance and lightening flashed, the rain followed. Finally, he saw her running across the back of the house behind the old barn. He called out, "Emma! Emma, wait!"

Then he suddenly stopped as fear gripped him in a way it never had before. He heard Emma scream a blood-curdling scream that washed over him like ice in his veins. Then, not hearing her at all frightened him more.

"Emma!" He screamed all the way to the well where, to his horror, he saw that the wood had broken through. Because she was upset, she hadn't seen, much less remembered, the small flag standing there in the ground in the rain and darkness. Just as he feared, he looked down and saw her at the bottom of the well.

"Emma, can you hear me?" he screamed. "Help! Somebody help me, please!"

He looked around and saw an old rusty chain in the shell of the old barn. He quickly hooked it to a post nearby to lower himself down the fifteen-foot shaft. There was barely room for him to fit, but he managed to finally make it down to Emma, where he found her unconscious, and thanked God she had not fallen over into the water. He quickly pulled her to himself and frantically kept calling her name. He slapped her face to hopefully jolt her back to consciousness.

"Emma, Emma, baby, it's me, Drew. Wake up, baby. Wake up." He was plagued with fear, and panic was beginning to set in because, although he knew CPR, there was not enough room to perform it in the confined space. There was only about four feet of water so he didn't have to try to stay afloat. He just held her as close as he could and kept talking to her. At last, she made a groaning noise, and relief rushed over him.

Crying, rocking her back and forth, he said, "Thank you, God. Thank you, God. Thank you, God. I thought I'd lost you."

She just moaned a little, but she was alive, and that was the important thing.

"Drew!" He heard his mom's yell from above. "Drew, are you okay?"

"Call 911! Emma fell in the well! She's hurt really bad!"

The mothers quickly made calls while Julie just stood in shock.

"Drew?" Emma spoke groggily. "What happened?"

"You were running, baby, remember? You didn't see the well and you fell through the old wood that was covering the top."

"Oh yeah. Ouch," she said after trying to move.

"Shh… just relax. I've got you. I won't let anything happen to you, Em."

"Drew, did you know?"

"About Julie being your sister? I promise, I had no

idea until today. I would never keep anything from you ever, but I wanted this night to be the special — one we'd never forget," he said brushing her hair out of her face and kissing her forehead.

"I think you got your wish. It *is* memorable." She almost laughed, but it hurt too badly.

"I bet this will leave the talk about the preacher in the dust," he said trying to keep her mind alert but off Julie.

She moaned again as she tried to lift up.

"Try not to move too much, baby. Not until the paramedics get here."

"Okay," she said, and she faded out again.

"Emma. Emma, stay with me. Emma,"

Her eyes opened again. Trying to keep her awake, he continued to talk. Drew knew every second counted, and the sooner they got out of there, the better. "You scared me, Em — thought I'd lost you."

"You can't lose me. I always come back." She half smiled.

"Well, where and when do you think we should get married?"

"On the front porch — this August. It's our month," she whispered with a half-smile.

"You got it. Yeah, August has always been eventful in our lives. Just look, today is August 1, and look how it turned out."

She tried to laugh again but stopped short with pain.

"Okay. Let's talk honeymoon."

"Easy. Yankees Game, New York."

"You sure know how to pick an opportune moment, you know that? Stay with me, Em."

"I love you, Drew," she barely whispered.

"I love you too, baby, so much." Then he kissed her again on the forehead. He was still scared that they wouldn't get her out in time, but he kept talking. "You know, I can even see you smile in the dark? I see it with my heart. Can you see with your heart, Em? Do you see us getting married? And having babies? I can't wait to have everything with you."

He was able to keep her awake and talking about their future and planning the wedding although she kept drifting in and out. Finally, the ambulance arrived along with the fire department — and Moose.

"How are ya'll down there?" Moose shouted.

"She's in and out of consciousness. She's hurt pretty badly. Hurry."

"Help is on the way, but you have to help us, Drew. You okay?"

"I'm fine, but let's get her out, now," he commanded.

It took some maneuvering, but finally, with Drew helping from the bottom of the well, they finally lifted her out. Then they sent something to lift him out as well.

"Drew, you're bleeding, man," Moose said.

"How's Emma?" He didn't even know he'd been cut.

"They are working with her, but dude, you seriously need to get your leg checked out."

"I am fine. Just take care of Emma." He closed his eyes and said, "My fiancée." Then, he cried for the first time. It scared him to think he'd almost lost her. Again.

Ella and Liza rode to the hospital together, but Drew rode in the ambulance with Emma.

No one discussed Julie. Emma didn't need that. She

needed all his love, and he knew love and hate could not reside in the same heart.

At the hospital, they whisked Emma to the back, and when the nurse at the front desk saw Drew's torn pants with blood all over him, she insisted he go back to get checked out as well. The only reason he agreed was because Emma was back there and that was the only way he could get to her.

Once he was in the back, he insisted he was okay and just had them wipe the blood away. They could not force him to take treatment but did give him some ointment and a Band-Aid. Soon he found Emma and was at her side.

It scared her when she saw his pants but he assured her he was okay. "Drew, I am so sorry I ran away like that. You saved my life tonight," she said through quiet tears and soft sniffs.

"Then we are even because you saved mine tonight too when you said you would be my wife." He kissed her hands.

"Thank you for saving me. I love you. I really love you." She drifted back out, but this time it was her pain medication.

He stepped back out in the ER waiting room so they could take her for x-rays.

Andrew Dalton finally arrived at the hospital in a panic with a tear stained face.

"Dad, Emma's fine. I'm fine."

"Thank God," Andrew said breaking down a little bit more out of sheer relief and engulfed his son in his arms.

He tried to explain what happened, and then the two moms walked up. They continued filling Andrew in with the details while Drew sat and took a much-needed deep breath. Right there in the waiting room while sitting in a chair, he broke down and cried like a baby in his mother's arms. All he could think of was how close he came to losing Emma. "She's got to be okay. Mom, she's got to be," he continued through the deep sobs. "I'd die if something ever happened to her."

About an hour passed, and the doctor came out and introduced himself. He extended his hand saying, "Hi, I am Dr. Benson."

He explained Emma's injuries. She had a slight concussion, a few cracked ribs, and a broken collarbone. That was the extent of her injuries, but they wanted to keep her overnight for observation. Then the doctor looked at Drew and asked, "You must be Drew. The man that jumped in to save her and that she keeps asking to see?"

"I jumped in, yes. I'm Drew. Drew Dalton, Emma's fiancée." He shook Dr. Benson's hand.

"She's a lucky lady to have someone love her that much. You really did save her life tonight. She would have drowned in that water had she been left there for a few more minutes."

Hearing those words made his blood grow cold once again. The one thing he could not imagine was his life without her. Being apart for all those years had been almost unbearable, but to live in a world where she no longer existed was inconceivable to him. The magnitude of it all was closing in on him. He was anxious to see her again and make sure she was okay.

He finally zoned back into the moment and answered the doctor. "I just had to. She's my Emma. Thank you for taking care of her."

The night was a complete blur to him. How had it all turned out like this? He knew all too well how, or *who*, had led them to this place.

"Well, hero," the doctor then said, bringing him back to the moment. "I think she'll be wanting to see you if you would like to go up and wait in her room for her. Oh, and I'll see that the nurse sends you some scrubs so you can change your clothes if you'd like."

"I'd appreciate that. Thanks again, doctor — for everything. " He shook his hand again and limped away.

Andrew, Liza, and Ella went to the room so they could say goodnight to Emma. They all wanted to kiss her and make sure she was okay before they left, but Drew was not budging. He had informed everyone to go home, and if he slept at all, it would be sitting in the chair directly facing her.

He did follow them into the hallway and gave strict orders for Julie not to come anywhere near Emma, *or* him. They all wanted to talk out the issue at hand, but each knew that after a near death experience like that, things seem to be put a little more into perspective.

Back in the room, Emma couldn't hold her eyes open any longer. Finally, they gave Drew the go ahead on letting her sleep. He leaned over her as she lay in the bed hooked up to all sorts of beeping machines and softly kissed her lips. "Goodnight my beautiful fiancée. I love you,"

She smiled and looked down at her ring and whispered, "Mrs. Drew Dalton." She smiled while saying with a slur, "I love you so much."

"Can I get you anything before you go to sleep?"

"Yeah, Sexy Dr. Drew."

"Anything, baby."

"Sing our song to me."

"You got it."

"And Drew, promise you'll stay with me. Don't ever leave me," she said barely audibly.

He gave her a quick kiss and touched her face looking intently at her. "Emma, now that, I *can* promise. I will always be right here for you, always. Goodnight, baby. Find me in your dreams."

He sat at her bedside, holding her hands, and sang to her until she fell asleep.

Chapter Twenty

"The world breaks everyone and afterward,
Many are strong in the broken places."
~Earnest Hemingway

When Emma opened her eyes, she saw Drew sitting in the chair beside her bed asleep with his head facing her. The events of the night were continually playing in her mind. She looked down at her ring and smiled thinking about how deeply in love she was and chose to stay in that memory a while. Her mind soon recounted the rest of the night, which resembled a slight nightmare. Julie Dalton Scott was her sister. Just where was she was supposed to file that piece of information?

As she was thinking, Drew opened his eyes. "Hey, fiancée. How do you feel? Do you need anything?"

"Well, honestly, I feel like I fell into a fifteen-foot well and broke a few things. Oh, I *did* do that, didn't I?" She laughed a little, although she was extremely sore.

"That's my, Emma — the one with a smart mouth." He leaned over and kissed her.

She then added in a soft, more serious tone as she looked into his eyes, "All I need is you with me always. Promise you'll never leave me."

He gently scooted her over and crawled into the bed with her, trying to be careful not to hurt her. "Baby, you're stuck with me. We're in this together — no matter what, remember? Together, we can get through anything." He kissed her forehead. "Em, know what I am the most excited about?"

"What?" she asked smiling.

"That you will be the last thing I see when I go to sleep at night, and the first thing I will see in the morning — that I will be able to hold you every single night — all night long."

"Drew, although last night was a tragic turn of events, it was the greatest night of my life. I'll never forget it. It was perfect," she said with a sleepy smile.

She leaned over with her good shoulder leaning against him. It wasn't long before she rooted about and was just under his arm where she seemed to fit best. She always felt that spot was designed for her. It made her feel safer than any place in the entire world.

Sometimes when she realized just how deep her love for him was, it simply made her heart ache. Lying there beside him, feeling the warmth of his body, she could almost feel herself melting over into him. Although they had not been through a formal ceremony, she knew they were already one.

The sun had not come up yet, so they fell asleep intertwined — physically, mentally, and spiritually.

The night shift nurses came in every now and then to check Emma's vitals but were extremely compassionate and let Drew stay in the bed with her.

About mid-morning, Emma woke up sweating. She

quickly realized it was not her; the heat was radiating from Drew. She put her hand to his face, and he was on fire. "Drew. Drew, are you okay?"

Groggily, he smiled at her and said, "Yeah, I am fine."

"You're burning up." When she slowly sat up her hand rubbed against his thigh, which quickly sent him reeling in pain.

"Drew, are you okay?" she asked and insisted on seeing his cut. "Drew. That looks awful! I'm calling the doctor." It may have been just a cut to begin with but Emma knew this was a serious wound. It was red, hot to the touch, and looked as if blisters were forming around it. "It's nothing, Em." When he tried to get up, he came right back down.

She watched as he lay back down on the bed and when he didn't try to move again, she knew something was terribly off.

"Drew, you are not okay. You don't look well, and look at your leg!"

"I'm probably just tired. That is just a scratch I got rescuing my bride-to-be—it's nothing," he said with a half-smile. "I do feel a little nauseous though. Don't worry," he said softly but unconvincingly, "I'll be alright."

She rang the nurse's station and a nurse came in moments later. The nurse looked at his wound and applied slight pressure, which caused him to reel with pain. Emma could tell by the nurse's expression that the cut alarmed her as well.

The nurse took his temperature and when it registered at 103.5, she immediately left to find the doctor on call. When Drew didn't protest, it scared

Emma even more.

The doctor came in shortly after the nurse left. The doctor was Dr. Benson, who had been on call the night before in the emergency room. "Drew, your fever is 103.5. Something is clearly going on with you."

The doctor walked over to the bed where Drew was lying." Let's have a look at the cut on your leg."

Emma helped remove his pants so they could examine the wound thoroughly and it seemed to have worsened. The color surrounding the cut was more of a violet color and had clearly spread in the short time it had taken the doctor to arrive. There was also a new development. As the doctor applied pressure, a liquid, that Emma thought resembled dirty dishwater, began to ooze from the wound.

The growing concern on Dr. Benson's face alarmed her, but the doctor didn't give her a chance to ask questions.

"We are going to run some blood work on you and start you on an IV. Our first priority is to get your fever down."

The next few hours became very intense as Emma was released from the hospital and Drew was admitted. Within two hours, he had gone from taking care of her and cuddling in her bed to being admitted to the ICU after tests showed a bacterial infection in his blood stream. The rusty chain he cut his leg on, mixed with the stagnant rainwater at the bottom of the abandon well was a toxic mixture to the gash in his leg. He was stable but under strict watch. Emma had gone from being in total euphoric bliss to devastating fear and anguish throwing her into a downward spiral that was breaking her down fast. She called their moms and Daddy D, and they were there back at the hospital within minutes.

Dr. Dupree was a specialist in internal medicine and called them all in the lobby of the ICU waiting room to explain Drew's condition. He told them that Drew had an infection, but for now, they had to wait on a few test results before they could pinpoint the type of infection. For now, he was comfortable resting, and his fever was down a degree. He ended by saying that all they could do was to pray and wait.

After the doctor left, Emma recounted to the family what happened in the past few hours, but it had happened so fast, it was all they could do just to process.

While the three sat in the waiting are, Emma felt she needed to talk about the previous night's revelations. "So, I wanted Drew here with me for this talk, but he's not. This may not even be the right time to even talk about this." She forced her tears to stop. "But, we may be here for a while, so somebody start talking. Now. I want to know about so many things. Like, how is it that no one bothered to tell me I have a sister? Julie, of all people? Mom, how could you keep this from me all these years?" She started crying again.

Ella and Liza wiped tears from their faces, but Daddy D remained stoic.

Silence fell among them until Emma spoke again with sarcasm, "Don't you all talk at once, okay?"

Finally, Liza began the discussion. She walked over to Emma wiping her own eyes with a tissue and took Emma's hands. "Baby girl, I cannot begin to know how you are feeling. I don't blame you for being so angry, but please let me say, I *am so* sorry. The timing of this…

well, it stinks. There was no good way to tell you, but let me try now. The summer I graduated from high school, we went on a senior trip to Greece — Athens actually. That is when I first met Carter. He was fun and handsome. I was so far away from home for the first time. On our last night there, well… you can figure it out. We had too much to drink. We knew it was a mistake. Later, I found out I was pregnant with Julie."

She blotted her eyes with the tissue as she paused. Ella came and sat by Emma, putting her hand on her back.

Then Liza continued. "Well, after I told my parents, there was no way your father would ever be allowed near any of us — or even know about Julie if my father had anything to say about it. They wanted me to go away and have an abortion or at least give her up for adoption, but I refused. I stayed out of school for a year, and my parents disowned me. I moved in with Pop and Mim — my father's parents. None of us ever heard from my parents again."

Liza stopped to cry for a moment, which broke Emma's already tender heart. Ella blotted her tears as well.

"I'm sorry," Liza said. "It still feels like it was yesterday. My parents moved to Arizona, and when Pop and Mim passed, everything in their trust was left to me. The money, the land — everything. The house you and Drew love so much is where they lived. Drew always loved it as much as his great-grandfather and grandmother did—as much as the two of you do. You feel the magic they always said was there.

"Anyway, when Julie was just two years old, I went back to school, and while I was there, I met Andrew, and I knew he was the one I wanted to spend my life with. He adored Julie and wanted to adopt her. During those two years, we told your daddy about Julie, and he had been in her life a little more. During that time, it was not common for unwed ladies to have babies, so we tried to keep it as low-key as possible. My grandparents were so gracious to your father and insisted that he remain in school.

"Well, after Andrew proposed, your daddy came and met with us. Out of his love for Julie, he signed the adoption papers. He always had a trust for her, and he paid for every dime of her college, but he loved and watched her grow up from the sidelines. But, what none of us expected…"

Her eyes filled up with tears again as Ella came over and hugged her friend and took over the story for her. "Emma, your daddy really was the true love of my life. We were crazy in love, and he told me about Julie soon after we started dating. He was never a deadbeat father or ashamed of her. When he told me about Julie, I wanted to meet her. He actually was doing some freelance work taking pictures of the waterfalls in the mountains, so on one of his trips we arranged to get together with the Daltons.

"I fell in love with them — their family — this town. It felt right. It took some getting used to, of course, but we all knew we belonged together. So, we *all* decided not to tell anyone about Carter being Julie's real father until Julie was eighteen, at least. By then, we felt she would be old enough to handle it, and with it being a small town, she could always leave if the talk started circulating. She was about to leave for college, and then…"

Ella fell completely apart, and Emma finished her sentence. "Dad was killed in the plane crash." She hugged her mom and Liza, and they held one another and cried.

Liza spoke again saying, "On the night of the plane crash, you and Drew were off playing somewhere. We thought Julie was with you two, but she wasn't, and she overheard us talking about Carter being her father. Something snapped inside her. We thought she was okay until she started taking it out on you. You were so young. We are so sorry we never told you or Drew until now. This is all our fault."

Andrew finally broke his silence. "You truly became like another daughter to us Emma, and I was the only father figure you had left. You became my little Emmy Em." Then tears formed in his eyes as well as he reached over and grabbed Emma. "We all love you three so much — more than you all will ever know, but it was our love for you, Emma, that sent Julie off."

By now, Emma was a complete wreck. She spoke through an avalanche of tears saying, "I… love you all, so… much," she said through a series of gasps for air. "I understand… and all that matters is now… and being with the ones you love, and letting them know it." She fell apart in Daddy D's arms. "Drew and I wasted so much time. I'm scared Daddy D. I'm so scared. I can't lose him."

"Aww, baby, you aren't going to lose him. He's gonna be just fine. You'll see." He dried her eyes with his handkerchief and told her again that it would all be okay. Emma wondered whom he was trying to convince more, her or himself.

Emma left them so she could wash her face and

take some pain medicine. The doctors had encouraged her to go home and rest, but she refused to leave, and no one really blamed her. She felt like half a person without Drew. At the very least, she felt safer knowing the rest of her was just a few feet away from her. He saved her. Now it was her turn to help save him. She was done running from pain and hurt. He was her life.

Chapter Twenty-One

"Blessed is the influence of one true loving human soul on another."
~George Eliot

Just as Emma walked back into the ICU waiting room, the family of Drew Dalton was called over the intercom to meet with the doctor just inside the double doors of the hall that led to the ICU patients.

"Drew is comfortable, but we know what we're dealing with now." The look on the doctor's face concerned them all. Emma felt her body going weak as he continued. "Basically, it's a form of Strep, but this type of Strep is different from other types because it's flesh eating. Drew cut his leg on the rusty chain, and then the open wound was exposed to the water down in the well, which was certainly contaminated."

"Drew has an extremely rare form of strep known as necrotizing fasciitis. This actually attacks soft tissue and spreads rapidly. The only way to treat this type is surgery. So much crucial time has been lost so we have ordered a CT scan to locate the exact location of the problem. This is aggressive and if it's not too far gone, the best case scenario is amputation. As I said, his fever has gone down to 102 for now, but it actually spiked at 104.5 before breaking. So the fever, nausea, chills, and dizziness are all from the infection.

"For now, our next step is get the scan done and into the OR but at the rate this is spreading, that's not a good thing. Time is not on our side."

Emma interrupted desperately. "What do you mean *not a good thing*? What will happen? He *is* going to be okay, right?"

"Time will tell, but we are the *most* concerned, at this point, with seeing what we are dealing with. We must act fast because it will be only a matter of time before it begins to attack the organs. Then…"

He stopped when Emma passed out. She was taken to another room, and he finished up with Drew's parents while her mom stayed with her.

When she woke up, Emma saw her mom at her side, and very weakly she said, "Mom, he can't…" She had no strength to talk. She spoke in chopped words but kept mumbling through groans. "He promised he'd never leave me. He *promised*, Mom."

"Emma, sweetie, would you like to go back and see him? The doctor said you can go back for a few minutes."

"Yes."

Ella helped her daughter to his room. "Honey, try to be strong for him, okay? I don't think he knows how sick he is."

Emma nodded her head and tried to be strong. Her mother let go of her, and she walked into his room alone. She was surprised to see him looking so good, considering, which made her feel better. By the way the doctor talked, she expected much worse.

"Hey fiancé." She reached over and kissed his cheek.

"Hey to you too, fiancée. How are you feeling?" he

asked, reaching out for her hand.

"Me? I am fine. Didn't you hear? I was rescued by a superhero last night." She really did feel stronger just touching him. Like always, they were stronger together than they ever were a part.

"Is that right?"

"That is a true story," she smiled and said. "Besides, you're the one in ICU, remember? I must say, I'm impressed with your superhero skills, but you shouldn't have come in after me. I would have been okay."

"Shh. I would do it over and over again if it would save my girl," he said weakly with his cute smile.

"Have I told you today how much I love you?" She smiled, kissed him, and ran her fingers through his hair overwhelmed that she loved him even more than she had the day before.

"Emma, do me a favor?"

"Anything."

"Could you ask Julie to come see me?"

"Julie? *Julie* is the reason all of this has even happened," she snapped. Then she suddenly remembered all the things their moms had just shared with her, and if the man she loved, who had just saved *her* life, wanted to see Julie, then how could she deny him that? She answered again much calmer. "I'm sorry. Of course I will. Anything you want." She kissed his hands. "I better go so our parents can come back before visiting time is up."

"Okay, but come back." It broke her heart to hear his voice growing weaker with each word, but he kept on talking very softly. "Hey, Emma, thanks for loving me so much." He stopped again to breathe and Emma realized his breathing was becoming more labored. He continued saying, "And Em, try not to be too angry at Julie. She doesn't love the way you do. She's broken in so many places. She needs her sister now, even if she doesn't know it yet."

With a smile on her face and fresh tears on the edge of her eyelids, she just nodded yes. Then she said through choked tears, "Loving you, that's what I do. It's kinda like breathing to me. I wouldn't know how not to." With another quick kiss, she left only to melt outside of his room and slide down the wall in tears.

Thankfully, when she walked into the ICU waiting room, she saw Jane. She walked over, and they hugged for a long time while they both cried.

"I brought you this. I didn't know what else to do," Jane said handing her an unsweetened tea from Mazi's. Emma tried to laugh.

"Thanks, Jane, and thanks for coming."

Sitting down, they continued the conversation. "How is he and how are you, sweetie?"

"Oh, I am fine but," she started with tears again. "I am really worried about Drew, though. This is really scaring me, Jane. His condition is serious. I mean, I *really* don't know if he'll be okay, and the thought of losing him after we just found our way back to each other…" She stopped to breathe and stop the flow of tears. "It's just all too much, ya know?"

"What are the doctors saying?"

"Jane, this could be fatal, " she said breaking down a little more with each word. Finally regaining her composure, she proceeded to tell Jane as much as she could remember. Everything was beginning to run together in her mind. She was in pain and totally exhausted, but she refused to leave Drew at the hospital. However, when their parents came back out, they insisted she let Jane drive her home so that she could shower and rest for a little while. It would be several hours before anyone was allowed to go back to see him again anyway. She fought them, but they insisted.

Jane gave Emma her space. After fixing a pot of coffee, she helped Emma upstairs to take a bath. Emma soaked in the tub and tried to relax but... How could she comprehend this all? Julie, Drew, and now this. She couldn't shake the feeling that something bad was going to happen. As she was getting out of the tub and reaching for her robe, she saw Drew's Yankee sweatshirt draped on the back of the chair. Emma put it on even though it was August and hugged herself into it as she crawled into her bed and curled up like a little child. Just when she didn't think she could cry anymore, the tears came once again, pouring like a water faucet. This was a nightmare. Why had she wasted so much time away from him? Time she would never have back. She was spent. In her wildest dreams she never imagined this. Physically she was limp from her own ordeal but that paled in comparison to how lost she felt without Drew. Time was wasting. The only thing on her mind was getting back to the hospital. The fear was rising in her so much that she could scarcely breathe.

Then her mom was at her door. "Knock, knock. You asleep?" she called.

"Hey, Mom," she said a little anxiously as she sat up. "Is Drew…?"

"He's fine, sweetie. He's stable, and his fever hasn't gone up any. There's no change."

An exhausted, tear wrenched Emma lay back down, sniffing Drew's cologne that still lingered deep in the fibers of the shirt that she was now glad she had never gotten around to washing.

"Emma…" her mother said as she crawled into the bed with her daughter. Ella ran her fingers through Emma's hair and patted her daughter's back. "Emma, when you were a little girl, this is always what we did when you were upset. Remember?"

Emma nodded her head yes.

"I told you there was a time in my life when I had to make some choices, remember? See, when I found out about Julie being Carter's daughter that actually took me some getting used to. Well, not at first. I appreciated and was touched that he was honest with me from the beginning, and he was so proud of her, but it was *after* I met her that was difficult for me.

"It was tougher than Liza ever knew. They had a past. They shared this beautiful little girl that he adored. How was I supposed to measure up to *that? Every day?* Carter let the final decision be mine. It was hard, but not once have I regretted it. In the end, my love for him outweighed my insecurities about his past with Liza. I was with the love of my life, and he was content to watch Julie grow up from the outside looking in.

"Then *you* came along, and our life was perfect. Then, when your father's plane went down, something inside me died and went away for a very long time. But, it was love that kept me going. Some call it magic, but it's love. Your father taught me to see the beauty in everything, and I know he taught you as well. If he were here right now, and I believe he is always with us, he'd want you to forgive Julie — to make things right.

"Her missing pieces have been ignored for some time now. She knew about them, but knowing that she had to repress it all… well, that kind of emotional torture can take a toll on anyone. My beautiful Emma, you have too much love in you to exchange it for that kind of darkness. She may choose to remain in her current place of denial and agony for your dad, for Drew, and for *you. But you,* my dear one, choose love. Don't ever forget to love."

Emma listened intently to her mom. She knew she was right, but she was too tired to respond. Ella kissed her daughter on the cheek and reached across to grab a blanket from the foot of the bed. She covered her little girl up and tucked her in just as she had when she was young.

"I am going to go downstairs and let you get some rest. I promise I will come wake you up in an hour and get you back to the hospital, but rest for a while, baby, just rest."

EMMA HEARD HER mother softly close the door. Her body then totally relaxed as her mind rested in her memories. She remembered her and Drew playing as children, the teenage years, when they fell in love, and her *favorite* part — the memories they made this past week. For the first time since they'd made love the night before, she took a deep breath and felt safe — like everything was going to be okay. She had fallen into the place between sleep and awake when she heard him. At first, she thought it was her imagination and then she knew she was dreaming. She didn't really care. She heard him again. It was him. Then, she heard him clearly call her name, "Emma."

"Drew." She ran and leapt into his strong arms straddling her legs around him like a little monkey. "What are you doing here? How? You're…"

"Em, Em, I'm fine. See?" He kissed her and swayed around dancing with her still strapped to him. Then he held her head in both hands.

They danced around, and then he sat on the bed with her still having her legs wrapped around him. She placed her head on his chest and rooted down just right until she was in that place designed just for her — a perfect fit under his arms. She lay there for a while just listening to his beautiful heartbeat and the music inside it — their music. Her senses where so full of Drew in a way she'd never experienced before. She felt him — she could smell him. The taste of his kiss even seemed heightened. Her favorite sensation, however, was how it felt holding him close to her. Somehow, she felt him deep inside her soul — more than ever before.

"Hey baby, you have got to let go sometime," he gently said.

"It feels so good to just hold you like this."

"I am right here. It's okay. I am so sorry you were so scared," he said tracing her cheekbones with his thumbs lightly giving her a quick kiss on the lips.

"I'm okay now, but you scared me so much. Don't ever leave me, Drew."

"Baby, do you not know by now that I will always be with you? I love you forever."

"Well, how did you get out of the hospital? What's up? Did the antibiotics work?"

"Shh. Shh." Ever so softly, he kissed her lips with his arms wrapped back around her. After the kiss he said, "Emma, I don't have much time, so listen to me…"

"What are you talking about? You just…" Fear struck her.

"Shh. Baby, listen," he whispered as he pushed the hair from her eyes with his fingertips. "Just listen. Em, I am going to have to go away."

"No," she said getting upset.

"Shh. Baby, don't cry. Listen. Listen. Let me explain," he said in a tone that calmed her. "Emma, will you do me a favor?"

"Of course."

"Okay then. Just hear me out." He sat her on the bed, and he got on the floor on his knees so they would be eye level. "Julie is not just *my* sister, she is *yours* too. Please, baby, please don't spend the rest of your life holding onto bitterness and hate. That's not you, Em. Love can't survive in a heart like that. I meant what I said when I said you were stuck with me, and when I told you our love was timeless, I meant that with all that I am. We have love just like those epic loves our English teachers used to make us read — those stories that we would discuss under the stars at *our* place."

She smiled remembering those days.

"Yeah, remember that?" He smiled back saying, "We really have that, Em." He kissed her hands as he continued. "Love like ours *never* dies — it *never* ends. It simply just *is*. People have to leave sometimes, but love never does. Please promise me, no matter what happens. Don't close your heart, because that's where I will always be — and when you feel your heart beat, that will be my love living inside of you. When you listen closely, you'll always hear the music, and Em, when you hear it, I want you to dance. I wish you love. I never want you to give up on your life. Live in your now, always, and no matter what, I will be between each of your breaths, *always* loving you — *always*."

Emma was breathing deeply not completely understanding what he was saying. She started to cry uncontrollably and clung to him. "No, Drew. No. I just got you back. You can't leave me. You promised..." Then, with her voice fading, she buried her face in his chest as he blanketed his strong, safe arms around her. She kept saying, mixed with heart wrenching tears, "You promised. You promised."

"Emma," he said with a calming tone that washed over her again. "Baby, I am *always* with you. I do promise, and please always know that I would rather have had this one week with you than a lifetime without you. My time with you has been worth my entire life..."

The tears were back, but this time in Drew's eyes as well.

"So Emma, if you really love me, show it by how you live, and please baby, never forget. I will love you forever, and there is not a single thing that will ever change that."

Then he gave her a real kiss — the kind that stirs the soul — the kind that remains with you for a lifetime. Then he picked her up and cradled her in his arms, breathing all of her into himself, holding her close just one more time. He placed her back on her bed kissing the top of her head. He pulled the covers over her and gave her a final kiss on the cheek. As she closed her eyes, she felt him brushing her hair with his hand, and she was totally relaxed again.

"Emma, Emma. Wake up honey."

Emma jumped up a little disoriented. She first looked around and said, "Drew?"

"Honey, Drew is not here, sweetie, remember? He's in the hospital."

"Mom… But…" She breathed deep and said, "I must have been dreaming, but it was so *real.*"

"Well, it's close to time for visiting hours, so I'll be ready when you are."

She quickly put on her shoes and decided to leave on his sweatshirt. With it on, she felt he was wrapped around her.

At the hospital, they knew something was wrong because it was still thirty more minutes before visiting hours and they called the family of Drew Dalton to the back.

Looking around, she didn't see his parents, so she went back and found Andrew, Liza, and Julie sobbing. Julie stood before Emma with eyes so swollen she could barely see them. Julie embraced Emma and said desperately, "I'm sorry. I'm so sorry. Can you ever forgive me?"

Emma simply looked as her tears flowed. When she said the words, she meant them. "It's okay, Julie. It's okay."

Then, she quickly left and went into Drew's little hospital nook behind the glass...

"Drew..."

Liza came in behind her and said, "Emma, the doctor just called us back a few minutes ago. They lost him for a minute but brought him back, so we could..." She could barely speak for the tears choking in her throat. "It was just too far gone. They waited too long, honey. He and Julie talked. Then we said our goodbyes. The last word he said was Emma." Liza left after saying, "Stay as long as you need to sweetheart..."

A devastated Emma walked over to the man she loved — the man she thought, a few hours ago, she'd spend the rest of her life with. She was numb as she walked over to his bed with a shattered heart. This could not be. Not Drew — not now. Why was this happening? After all this time? She stood next to the bed and touched his face. He looked so peaceful, but panic took over, and she began to cry out his name.

"Drew, don't leave me. Please wake up. Drew, it's me — Emma,"

Faintly, he said with eyes barely open, "Em — been waiting for you."

Kissing his face repeatedly she said, "I love you, baby. I love you forever, I promise. I promise to always make sure my heart is a place you can always live. Just please, don't leave me. *Please,* Drew," she pleaded through gasps for breath, now sobbing. "Stay *here* with *me…"*

He said, "I love you, Em," and he closed his eyes.

She fell over his body crying. Then she looked up and touched his face. She kissed his lips softly and said, "I love you, Drew." She patted his heart, crawled over into his bed, under his arm — one more time. Crying, she whispered, "Find me in your dreams."

She stayed there until they made her leave the room. At least he was still breathing. There was always hope.

Chapter Twenty-Two

*"Eventually you will come to understand that love heals everything,
And love is all there is."*
~Gary Zukav

THE DAYS TURNED into months. The months turned into years, and soon, five years had passed. So much had changed, yet so much remained the same. Dreams were finally coming true, and this day would be one of much awaited celebration.

As the guests arrived, Emma just stood from a distance taking it all in. It was finally time for the dedication of the finished projects. The renovations were completed on the house and the amphitheater. The grove had *finally* been given an official name and all would be part of the program on this lovely, April morning.

The weather was perfect. Ms. Ella had the flowers just right — yellow daffodils. Mazi had the food perfectly placed — and plenty of it. Darcy Spenser Scott had helped by setting white chairs over the front lawn right in front of the makeshift stage, which, of course, was the front porch in which Emma had insisted upon — and her sister, Julie, made sure the stage was set up properly and ready to go — bossing everyone along the way, no doubt because that is what she always did best.

Emma couldn't believe Jane and Alec were missing all of this, but love does trump all, and they had put off their honeymoon long enough. Alec left the advertising agency after marrying Jane and moved to Leyton and started his own advertising agency. They were married inside the mansion on Christmas Eve but had to put off their Fiji honeymoon until business was up and running. Emma joked that he married on Christmas Eve to squeeze Jane in as a last minute tax write off. She was so happy for her friends.

The big event was planned to coincide with the annual Flywheel Festival, which was certainly when the board for the Dalton Foundation had hoped it would be. There was no better time to promote the town of Leyton than the weekend of the Flywheel, so everyone was happy.

Mrs. Liza and Daddy D were chasing Benji's little sister, Ashby Claire. She was just learning to walk, and she insisted on walking everywhere as fast as her chubby little legs would go. The family was scattered throughout the premises and were all on stand-by in case they saw the little one going rouge.

Sheriff Calvin Scott was off for the day so he and John were the gophers on call. So far, they had been the busiest of all. Calvin walked over to let Emma know that the preacher had arrived so they could begin when she was ready. Emma was so relieved they finally had gotten a new preacher. This man truly loved people, and he was very involved in the heart of the community. He was welcomed by all and was a breath of fresh air.

"Thanks for the heads up, Calvin," Emma said looking around the yard. "Have you, by chance, seen

Drew anywhere? It's time to start, and we have to go sit on the stage. Julie insisted we all three sit up there," she said laughing and rolling her eyes.

"Drew is entertaining all the children on the side patio, as usual," he replied with a laugh and shake of his head.

"Honestly, that Drew. I better round up the troops, then. Wish us luck," she said.

She spotted Julie in the distance and motioned to her that it was time. Then she stepped over to where the kids were playing and smiled. She remembered her and Drew as children playing in that very spot — him pestering her as she pretended not to like it. She stood there a moment letting the echo of time take her for a moment.

"Stop, Drew. I am trying to write these lines," a young Emma protested.

"'Stop, Drew. I am trying to write these lines.' Oh come on, Em. Let's play," he teased back.

In her mind's eye, she could still see him coming up behind her plopping a frog down right on her paper. She smiled as she watched her young self, chasing him all over the place in her mind. She treasured every memory they ever made. Today especially.

She allowed the memory to linger a little longer, and then she smiled to herself and whispered, "Yeah, you are right. We *are* timeless." Then she finally called out, "Drew! Drew Dalton, it's time. Come on or we are going to be late for our own event. Come on, honey, it's

THE *Point*

time. We have to go take our seats on the stage."

"Mommy, it is not a stage. It's a porch," Drew said.

"Well, it may look like a porch to you, young lady, but trust me, it's a stage," she said smiling at her beautiful four-year-old daughter. As they took their seats, Emma shared one of the quicker stories about how she and her daddy played there when they were little.

The mayor welcomed everyone on behalf of the board, and the preacher delivered the invocation. Then, it was time for Emma to speak. She took a deep breath and smiled at her daughter and her sister who already had tears forming in her eyes.

Emma, on the other hand, seemed to have an extra strength about her today. She had a beautiful little girl that looked just like her daddy, an amazing older sister whom she dearly loved, and she had just finished her first novel, The Point. It had been healing for her to write it, and now the entire world could read about the epic love story of her and Drew. They really were timeless and now even in print.

She stood before the microphone exactly where young Benji, or Ben as he preferred to be called now, had instructed her to stand. Just before she spoke her first word, she placed her hand over her heart and felt the beat of it, and knew she did not stand there alone.

"Good morning, everyone. Again, I would like to welcome each of you here today at Ashton Point, and thank you all for coming. Five years ago, Drew Dalton approached me about an idea he and I had dreamed about as children. That was a busy time in my life, and more than once, I tried to turn him down, *but* anyone that had the privilege to know Drew can tell you that he didn't comprehend the word no.

"So reluctantly, I took a leave of absence from my job, and with a leap of faith, I joined Drew in making our childhood dream a reality. As children, we fell in love with this house believing in its magic and being captivated by its charm. Many days, we performed on this very porch I am standing on now for our friends, family, and imaginary audiences."

She looked and gave a wink to her daughter, Drew, when she heard her giggle. Julie placed her arm around her as Emma continued.

"We were just two little kids with great big dreams. Although we grew up and moved away for a while, the magic we discovered here remained — even when we didn't. The magic I keep referring to is that of a child's imagination, or that of a first love — of sunsets and sunrises. All linger here through the echoes of time and space. It's the magic called love.

"To the right of this lawn, you see the beautiful magnolia tree standing strong and tall. It was planted in 1938 by James Sinclair Hastings II. Drew once told me that he actually planted *two* magnolias, one on each side of the entrance of the walkway to represent the love he and his wife, Clara shared. He planted them the day they moved in this lovely home. Being planted so closely together, eventually, their root systems intertwined. They still looked like two separate trees, but actually, they were one sharing the same nutrients for survival.

"One night however, a strong storm hit the city of Leyton and destroyed one of the two trees, leaving the other to stand alone. Today, we see only one tree, but the heart of this tree — what keeps it alive, the part not visible to our eyes, is still intertwined with the fallen one. Actually, this tree stands taller and stronger because the other tree is gone. The tree left the most important thing — its heart. Now, all that energy and strength can be poured into the growth of the one that remains standing while the other exists inside just beneath the surface.

"Like that tree, I stand alone before you today, but I am not alone. The love of my life, Drew Dalton, stands before you as well. He is the strength that kept me going after his death five years ago, and even now, after all these years, he still is. He left within me, not only his strength, but also his passion for life — his wonderful, loving heart — his magic, his love. He lives on each day through this place — through our friends, our family — and especially through our little girl. Drew believed that dreams could always come true, and I know he is here with us watching *our* dream become a reality.

"One of his favorite quotes was written by Johann Wolfgang Von Goethe which says, 'We are shaped and fashioned by what we truly love.' Well, look around you, and you will see everything Drew truly loved because everything you see here was from his heart.

"In closing, I would like to say that this place represents the pure magic of just how powerful love is. In family, friendships, forgiveness, healing — love is the root of it all, and that is exactly what all dreams are made of — love.

"I would like Julie and Drew to join me now as we hold up ribbons representing each dedication site. In my hand, I hold Ashton Point. Our daughter, Drew Elizabeth, holds The Drew Dalton Memorial Amphitheatre, and our sister, Julie Dalton Scott, holds the Carter Ashby Grove ribbon, which, of course, is in memory of our father. So hand in hand, we stand before you dedicating these three locations to the town of Leyton and to all that they represent. All the joy, all the dreams, and all the love you have yet to discover. So now, may you all go find your magic. Thank you."

The crowd stood, and the applause echoed far beyond Ashton Point, so far that she was certain Drew could hear them in heaven.

Little Drew was just glad it was over and went to find Ben so she could play with the microphone. Julie and Emma however, stood in an embrace filled with tears of thanksgiving and love. As they were leaving, Emma told Julie she'd catch up in a minute as the guests flowed into the great room for refreshments. Emma glanced at the stage and for a minute, she caught a glimpse of her and Drew just sitting under the big white columns, dreaming. She softly said, "I love you, Drew. We did it." She wiped a single tear away as she joined the guests.

A few hours later, as they were cleaning up, Ella came into Emma's office, which was on the second floor facing the balcony. At the close of every work day, Emma stood and looked over the railing before she left, the castle of her dreams...

"Emma, here is your child who is covered from head to toe in mud," her mother said, feigning aggravation.

Emma laughed remembering how fun the mud around there was. "Mom, she just appreciates a good mud bath." She winked. "We are going to head home, bathe, and change clothes, but we'll meet you all at the festival later. What's the theme for tonight?"

"Eighties, I think."

"Perfect," Emma said with a smile as she once again thought of Drew.

Ella walked over to Emma and gave her a hug saying, "I am so proud of you, honey, and I know your daddy and Drew are watching over this day with just as much love and pride as anyone. I love you, kiddo."

"I love you too, Mom."

As Ella was leaving, she smiled as she spied Drew's old guitar that Emma kept beside her desk.

"Emma, can you even play this thing?"

Emma replied, "Yeah. I can play one song." She smiled as if she were sharing that private little joke. She then looked at her filthy child and said, "Come on, little lady, let's go clean you up."

They drove the Mustang home. When they arrived at the cabin, they got out and Drew shouted, "Mommy, look! Look at all the yellow flowers! Can we go pick some? Please…"

"I'd love to, baby," she said.

They ran into the field, picked some of the daffodils, and placed a few in their hair. Then Emma asked Drew, "Would you like to dance?"

"Oh, Mommy. You're silly. There's no music,"

Emma bent her knees so she was eye level with Drew. She placed Drew's ear to her heart and said, "Oh baby, yes there is. Listen."

And they danced.

The End

Epilogue

You can shed tears that he is gone,
Or you can smile because he has lived.
You can close your eyes and pray that he'll come back,
Or you can open your eyes and see all he's left.
Your heart can be empty because you can't see him,
Or you can be full of the love you shared.
You can turn your back on tomorrow and live yesterday,
Or you can be happy for tomorrow because of yesterday.
You can remember him only that he is gone,
Or you can cherish his memory and let it live on.
You can cry and close your mind,
Be empty and turn your back,
Or you can do what he'd want,
To smile, open your eyes, and go on.
~ David Harkins~

About The Author

BORN AND REARED in Mississippi, Lori Harrington loves the South and all the charms its borders provide. As a teenager, Lori was interested in writing, but like many southern girls, she was swept away by a southern gentleman. Lori married and had children, allowing her dream of writing to become stagnant. 31 years later, Lori and her husband have three children and two grandchildren. Blissfully happy, Lori has experienced enduring love her entire life, and yet, pushed aside dreams don't die.

For Lori, writing is a constant friend. She didn't choose to be a writer—writing is a part of who she is, who she has been, and who she has become. Lori loves to create, and her passion immersed her in music, theater, and writing. She also has a burning desire to help women overcome obstacles, a characteristic she attributes to her southern roots.

Lori cherishes time with her family, and she is blessed to have support for her dreams and aspirations. Though a first time author, Lori believes that dreams can be achieved through hard work, persistence, and faith.

Acknowledgments

I, FIRST, WOULD like to thank God for creating this incredible imagination in me and finally leading me to the place to channel it.

I secondly want to thank Hank, Kati, Marykelli, and Walt for putting up with me the past few hectic years and encouraging me no matter what.

I also want to thank my parents, my family, and my friends for being amazing cheerleaders during this journey—especially my number one cheerleader, my mama.

Lastly, I want to graciously thank Kimberly, my editor and my friend. If I had not met you, this would not be happening. Thanks for giving new life to my dusty old dream. I will forever be grateful.

Also From Blue Tulip Publishing

BY MEGAN BAILEY
There Are No Vampires in this Book

BY J.M. CHALKER
Bound

BY ELISE FABER
Phoenix Rising
Dark Phoenix
Phoenix Freed
From Ashes
Blocked

BY STEPHANIE FOURNET
Butterfly Ginger
Leave A Mark

BY MARK FREDERICKSON & MELORA PINEDA
The Emerald Key

BY JENNIFER RAE GRAVELY
Drown
Rivers

BY LESLIE HACHTEL
The Dream Dancer

BY E.L. IRWIN
Out of the Blue
The Lost and Found

BY J.F. JENKINS
The Dark Hour

BY AM JOHNSON
Still Life
Still Water
Still Surviving
Now & Forever Still

BY A.M. KURYLAK
Just a Bump

BY KRISTEN LUCIANI
Nothing Ventured
Venture Forward

BY KELLY MARTIN
Betraying Ever After
The Beast of Ravenston
The Glass Coffin

BY NADINE MILLARD
An Unlikely Duchess
Seeking Scandal
The Mysterious Miss Channing
Highway Revenge
The Spy's Revenge

BY MYA O'MALLEY
Wasted Time
A Tale as Old as Time

BY LINDA OAKS
Chasing Rainbows
Finding Forever
The Way Home

BY C.C. RAVANERA
Dreamweavers

BY GINA SEVANI
Beautifully Damaged
Beautifully Devoted

BY ANGELA SCHROEDER
The Second Life of Magnolia Mae
Jade

BY T.C. SLONAKER
The Amity of the Angelmen

BY K.S. SMITH & MEGAN C. SMITH
Hourglass
Hourglass Squared
Hourglass Cubed

BY MEGAN C. SMITH
Expired Regrets
Secret Regrets

BY CARRIE THOMAS
Hooked

BY LORI THOMAS HARRINGTON
The Point

BY NICOLE THORN
What Lies Beneath
Your Heart Is Mine

BY RACHEL VAN DYKEN
Upon a Midnight Dream
Whispered Music
The Wolf's Pursuit
When Ash Falls
The Ugly Duckling Debutante
The Seduction of Sebastian St. James
An Unlikely Alliance
The Redemption of Lord Rawlings
The Devil Duke Takes a Bride
Savage Winter
Every Girl Does It
Divine Uprising

BY KRISTIN VAYDEN
To Refuse a Rake
Surviving Scotland
Living London
Redeeming the Deception of Grace
Knight of the Highlander
The Only Reason for the London Season
What the Duke Wants
To Tempt an Earl
The Forsaken Love of a Lord
A Tempting Ruin
A Night Like No Other
The One

BY JOE WALKER
Blood Bonds

BY KELLIE WALLACE
Her Sweetest Downfall

BY C. MERCEDES WILSON
Hawthorne Cole
Secret Dreams

BY GRACIE WILSON
Beautifully Destroyed

BY K.D. WOOD
Unwilling
Unloved

BOX SET — MULTIPLE AUTHORS
Forbidden
Hurt
Frost: A Rendezvous Collection
A Christmas Seduction

BLUE TULIP
PUBLISHING

www.bluetulippublishing.com

Made in the USA
Charleston, SC
26 November 2016